Love, Lies & Consequences trilogy

Book One : Love

By

Susan Elle

For

Ursula Publishing UK

Love, Lies & Consequences
Book One : Love
Text Copyright © 2013
By Susan Elle
Ursula Publishing UK
All Rights Reserved.

Cover Photograph
© Yuri Arcurs/Dreamstime.com

ISBN 978-1-910753-05-7

Other Books by Susan Elle

The Sara Colson Trilogy
Sara's Child
Sara's Loss
Sara's Shame
All the above also available as audio books.

Catherine Colson-Sayers Investigations
(CCS Investigations)
Book 1 : Missing
Book 2 : The Chosen
Book 3 : Travis
Book 4 : Deleted

Tempest
Broken

Love, Lies & Consequences Trilogy
Book One : Love
Book Two : Lies
Book Three : Consequences

Langdon Trilogy
Heart & Home
Heart of a Lion
Heart of Stone
http://www.susan-elle.com

Table of Contents

<u>PROLOGUE</u>

If she doesn't hurry up Zoe is going to be late for her job interview, and this is the best one out of the bunch she has gone for.

"Mum, can I please borrow a pair of tights – I just snagged these and they're sure to go into a hole the minute I'm out the door."

"Zoe Benson, I swear I've never seen you in such a state," her mother smiles as she holds out a replacement pair of tights. "You will be fine. If you don't get this job there will be others – and it'll be their loss!"

Hopping around, struggling into the new tights, Zoe at last gets them on and gives her mum a hug.

"That's what all mum's say – but I love that you think so!" *Now I just have to convince the interview panel!*

Birmingham is such a fast paced city that the traffic is

heavy even mid-morning. She manages to make it to the Johnson Construction Company car park with 10 minutes to spare – usually she likes to arrive for interview at least 20 minutes early to give herself time to calm down and tidy up. But today she will just have to dive straight in.

This is interview number 20, the same number as her age. *Ha! Maybe that will be my lucky omen. Or not, if I don't get myself in there toot-sweet!*

Straightening her skirt, Zoe tries not to wobble in her new four inch heels. She isn't tall and feels they give her stature if not grace. But she's aiming for both just now.

"Good morning, may I help you?" the receptionist asks politely as she enters the outer office.

"My name is Zoe Benson; I'm here for an interview for the secretarial post."

The receptionist smiles and waves a hand to indicate a small row of nearby chairs. "Take a seat and I'll let them know that you're here."

Ok, you're here on time, and it's just another job that you're not going to get so why be nervous. Just go in there and be yourself!

"Ms Benson," the receptionist smiles over to her, "if you'd like to take the lift up to the 15th floor, there will be someone there to show you the way."

Reaching across the desk, Zoe holds out her hand then

grins when the older woman takes it. "Wish me luck, I've a feeling I'm going to need it. I'm so nervous."

Delighted by the young woman's open manner, the receptionist returns her grin and tells her, "I don't think you'll need it but, good luck anyway."

Ok. Ok. 15th floor here I come!

Stepping into the lift, Zoe checks her reflection in the full length mirror someone has thoughtfully had fitted to the back wall. She straightens her already straight skirt, pulls her fingers through her long auburn hair and wipes the corners of her lipstick and...

"Hello, Ms Benson," a beautiful man with the most beautiful voice speaks to her back as she is still turned to the mirror wall, busily checking her reflection.

Turning quickly, Zoe overbalances on her four inch heels and falls into the strangers arms.

"Oh my god! I'm so sorry," she tells the man who is now holding her against his length to steady her. "I don't think I've ever been this nervous before an interview, I've turned into a complete klutz – sorry."

Holding her away from him, the stranger gives her a killer smile that does nothing to still her racing heart.

"Why are you so nervous – aren't you up to the job?" he smiles playfully.

"Well, yes, I just finished business school with top

grades – but I want this one so bad...it's offering the best opportunity to put my Diploma to good use and the company has a good rep as an employer." She drops her voice to a conspiratorial whisper, "I have this problem, when I'm nervous, like now, I blather – I can't stop myself. It's like verbal diarrhoea without a stop tap!" *Oh god! Did I just say that out loud!*

"Sorry – that was graphic...way too graphic." Holding out her hand, Zoe returns his broad grin and introduces herself, "Hi, I'm Zoe, nice to meet you."

"Hi, I'm Palmer Johnson, nice to meet you, too!"

CHAPTER ONE

With her head on the steering wheel, Zoe sits in the Johnson Construction car park and just waits for the world to cave in on her.

Of course, it does nothing of the sort but she's sure it will, given time.

She has just suffered the worst interview ever. Having first, quite literally, fallen into the boss's arms and then cheerfully told him that she suffers from verbal diarrhoea. Not something any boss would want to find out about his prospective secretary.

But at least he'd been nice about it. The interview was good, once she'd extricated her size 4's from her big mouth, Zoe had actually performed quite well.

But that's because you knew you'd already blown it! There was no point holding back after the fiasco by the lift. Damn it! I really wanted this one!

Lifting her eyes, she looks all the way up the very tall building to the offices on the top floor. Somewhere up there are people who are right now deciding her future – what she wouldn't give to be a fly on that particular office wall.

Palmer is laughing to himself, sipping his black coffee and contemplating the human dynamo that has just finished interviewing for the secretarial vacancy.

She was a bundle of energy full of good ideas - once she got over the shock that she had, quite literally, just fallen for the boss!

He couldn't help it, he was still laughing to himself when he walked over to his office window and looked down into the company car park.

And there she is! All suited up and on her way home. See you soon, Zoe Benson. I'm looking forward to it.

"Oh, mum!" Zoe is grateful for the hug her mother gives her as soon as she sees her daughter's disappointed face. "I couldn't have blown it any bigger than I did!" And she explains about tumbling out of the lift and falling full length into her prospective boss's arms. "He was actually really nice about it. But at the end of the day, they're looking for a professional person – I did not come across, in any way, as being a professional do-it-all secretary!"

"I'm sure it wasn't as bad as all that," her mum

reassures Zoe, and guides her into the kitchen for a nice cup of tea. "Just sit down and I'll put the kettle on, then we can look at the new job vacancies together. Forget about this one and chalk it up to experience – and a lesson on how not to exit a lift!"

They both laugh, seeing the funny side of things is something they are both good at and it has served them well over the years.

Zoe's father had left her mother when she had been a baby. She has no memory of him and has never let it bother her.

After all, her mum more than makes up for the cheating father who hadn't wanted her in the first place. And what is the point of dwelling on the past when the future is so full of promise.

That has always been their motto. They live on the premise that tomorrow is another opportunity to do something that you didn't get to do today – a second chance!

"Here you go, nothing like a nice cup of tea to soothe the way," Carly Benson smiles and takes a seat at the dining table with her daughter. "Have you found anything interesting?"

"Hmm...I think I'll take a look at this later," Zoe folds the newspaper and pushes it to the middle of the table.

"Everything I look at just looks boring compared to what I just missed out on. Maybe they'll look more enticing once I've gotten over it a bit."

Giving Zoe's arm a reassuring rub, Carly smiles and sips her tea without comment. It doesn't do to push at her daughter; it's only ever served to make her go in the opposite direction in the past. So, being wise in the way that mothers usually are, Carly lets the matter rest.

"Fancy a walk?" Zoe asks restlessly. "It's a glorious day and I'm going to go crazy if I don't walk off some of this disappointment!"

"Were you planning to go in those?" Carly asks, looking down at Zoe's 4 inch heels.

"Not on your life!" And she kicks them off under the dining table and walks out into the hallway to pull on a pair of low heeled sandals.

"Ready?" Carly smiles and gets a smile in return.

"You bet – just let me get my bag."

Dashing back to the dining table, Zoe picks up her bag and hooks it over her shoulder.

"Ok. Let's go!"

The sun is high and hot. It isn't too far a walk into the plaza where modern cafés mingle with shops, their outside tables providing ideal stop-offs for admiring recent purchases.

Groups of girls, groups of guys, couples and the odd singles; all are enjoying the café culture that is so rife in this part of town.

"Let's walk through to the park," Zoe suggests, her arm tucked into her mum's and her smile becoming less pained.

How can anyone stay miserable in a place like this? I love the buzz and vibe of city life – and I'll have something to celebrate soon enough!

Walking through to his PA's office, Palmer gives her a frown of concern. "Are you feeling alright – you're not doing anything scary are you?"

Laughing, Patricia Hayes, Palmer's current PA, shakes her head. "No, I'm not going into labour – my back just gives me twinges sometimes." How like Palmer to be concerned for her; ever since he'd found out she was pregnant he'd lightened her duties to the max. "So, do you want me to phone Ms Benson?" she asks, thinking this was what Palmer had come in for.

"Oh, no, I'll do that in a minute – I just wanted to give you this," and he hands over a plain white envelope.

Looking confused, Patricia opens it and very nearly keels over.

"Hey, hey – what is it about females today? Have you all been on the falling down water?"

Helping her into her seat, Palmer watches her regain her sensibilities.

"Palmer, you have already been more than generous...this is...this is wonderful!" she manages finally.

"You've always put the time in, whatever and whenever I've needed you," he tells her. "I'm sorry that you won't be coming back after junior is born, but I don't really blame you."

"Oh, Palmer!" Patricia stands and throws her arms around her boss's neck and has to stifle a flood of threatening tears. "You hurry up and find yourself a decent girl to settle down with then you'll be having little Junior's of your own!"

Walking back to his office, Palmer can only wish. He's always loved kids, but the right girl to have them with just seems to be eluding him.

"Ok...Zoe...Zoe...ah...Zoe Benson," he mutters as he leafs through the application forms on his desk. Smiling, he dials the number on the form and imagines her surprise.

"Oh, hell – could you hold this for me?" Zoe gives her mum the ice-cream cone she's just started to enjoy and fishes around in her shoulder-bag for her mobile.

"Hello...oh...oh no," she cries as the mobile is jostled out of her hand and hits the grass. Grabbing at it quickly

Zoe returns it to her ear and hears a familiar chuckle. "Hello, are you still there?"

"I certainly am, Ms Benson – are you free to speak?" Palmer asks, not able to make out from the background noise where Zoe might be.

"I'm...yes...that's fine – I'm in the park and an enthusiastic jogger just knocked my phone out of my hand," she explains with a nervous giggle.

It brings an answering chuckle from Palmer as he imagines her plight. "Well, I hope you're alright – I actually called to offer you the job..." but then he has to quickly hold the phone away from his ear as a piercing scream pours out from it.

"Oh my goodness – you surprised me so much – I'm sorry about that!" she tells him breathlessly. "My mum is standing right next to me and thinks I've completely lost my mind. Oh no, maybe I have – did you really just offer me the job?"

Laughing now, Palmer leans back in his seat and grins into the phone. "I most definitely did. Are you still keen to start?" he asks, thinking of his current, very pregnant PA.

"Very. I can start as soon as you need me," Zoe tries to sound keen but not too desperate, and fails completely.

"Take it easy," Palmer tries to calm her youthful exuberance, "the job is yours, just tell me when would be good for you?"

Taking a much needed breath, Zoe looks at her mum and uses her calming presence to focus.

"Ok. I'm calm and I really can start as soon as you'd like," she assures him. "I doubt your current PA has long till she goes on maternity leave, so the sooner I start the longer I'll have to pick her brains for the essentials."

"Good enough," Palmer agrees, liking her go-get-'em attitude. "Be here tomorrow at 8.30 – I'll show you around and Patricia can help you settle in."

"I'll be there...and thank you," she breathes out slowly, trying to take it all in. "I won't let you down."

Turning stunned eyes to her mother, Zoe suddenly lets out another ear-piercing scream that has passers by jumping away from her.

<u>CHAPTER TWO</u>

Pulling up in the car park, Zoe has to reign in her grin. She caught her reflection in the car door before unlocking it on her mother's drive. She had looked manic – scary really, she thought. But she just couldn't help it. Today is the first day in her dream job!

Going in to the small ground floor reception office, Zoe's grin couldn't be controlled as she once again shakes hands with the receptionist.

"I made it – I start work for Mr Johnson today," she tells her, and the receptionist gives her a more sedate but warmly welcoming smile.

"Welcome on board," she tells Zoe. "I'm Meryl, we'll be seeing quite a bit of each other I imagine."

"Is it ok for me to go up, Meryl?" she asks politely.

"They're expecting you – do you remember the way to Mr Palmer's office?"

Nodding, Zoe considers the woman's unusual way of addressing Palmer Johnson.

"Ok then. I'll ring up stairs and tell them you're on your way."

Mr Palmer – is that how he prefers to be addressed? A bit unusual, but maybe he's trying to do away with the formalities; although, she did still tag on the Mr.

This time when she steps out of the lift, Zoe makes sure that she is facing the doors and that she is able to walk off of it without falling at someone's feet.

However, there was no 'someone' to worry about. The corridor is long and empty, and she just hopes that she remembers the way correctly.

Knocking on a partially open door, Zoe pushes it wider and hears a familiar voice, and one she doesn't recall.

"Connor, I need you on site – I'll be there in a couple of hours and then we'll get the bulk of the ground work out of the way."

Then she hears another male voice, only this one sounds angry. "It's time you got a foreman – I could help out in the office, pricing up jobs the way you do," he whines, something Zoe doesn't find attractive in a man.

"That's what I pay you for, damn it! Now get on site and earn your damned salary like everyone else!"

Before Zoe can clear the way, a fierce eyed young man

in work gear bulldozes his way past her and is gone in a blink.

Moving cautiously forward to the open inner office door, Zoe peeks into the room and gets another surprise.

"Mr Johnson...I hardly recognised you," she stares open mouthed at his less formal attire.

He is wearing a vest top with a short sleeved shirt left open over it. His jeans are well worn and the leather tool belt tells her he isn't planning on being in the office much today.

Pushing an angry hand through his blond hair, Palmer looks across at his new PA. "As you may have heard, I plan to be on site today. That means getting my hands dirty and my old work gear on."

Then he smiles, this is her first day on the job and she's already heard him and his brother fighting. *Well, she might as well get used to it! It's not going to be the last time she hears us go at it!*

"The young man who didn't bother to introduce himself is my brother, Connor Johnson," he informs her and feels himself start to relax. "He works for me on site – unfortunately he doesn't think manual labour suits him so he throws a wobbly every now and then."

Her smile returning as his mood lifts, Zoe finds herself relaxing also. "You look like you're ready to do some manual work yourself," she smiles, the brilliance of it twinkling in her sparkling brown eyes.

Palmer is dazzled by that smile, and finds himself taking an unconscious step towards her. "Unlike Connor, I enjoy the physical aspects of the job. Getting down and dirty is what it's all about," he grins.

Zoe has to gulp in air, he is way taller than her meagre 5'5" and his muscles are mind-boggling under the open shirt.

"I suppose so," she manages to say. "The most down and dirty I ever got was playing mud-pies in the garden – my mum says I loved it!"

A roar of laughter erupts from Palmer, and Zoe finds herself laughing more from nerves than humour.

"You're a rum one and no mistake," he tells her, and then spots Patricia come into the outer office. "Patricia, I'm glad I caught you before I left. Zoe is here to learn from the master and I'm off to the Dersinger site." He walks through then lifts a hand of farewell, "I might be back, but maybe not – depends how well the job is going. Have a good first day."

Left staring after him open mouthed, Zoe eventually turns to find Patricia smiling knowingly at her.

"He's a looker, isn't he? I've known Palmer and Connor for years, even before I worked here – but they still have an effect on my blood-pressure," she laughs.

"I feel like I just got hit over the head with a mallet," Zoe says, giving her head a small shake to clear it. "Did you hear Palmer and Connor earlier? I'm afraid I walked in, in the middle of it."

Pursing her lips in annoyance, Patricia moves behind her desk and takes her usual seat, pointing to another for Zoe.

"You'll need to grow some thick skin," Patricia warns. "Every time they get together those two have at each other. And I'm not speaking out of turn, or gossiping. You need to know what you're in for."

Inside Zoe cringes. "Does it happen often then?"

Nodding, Patricia makes herself as comfortable as her advanced pregnancy will allow. "I'm going to give it to you straight – you'll hear rumours but that is all they are! The truth is both men got a nice inheritance when their Grandmother passed away about 8 years ago. Palmer invested his, continued his apprenticeship in construction then started his own business. But Connor, who is two years younger at 24, didn't save or invest any of his money."

Turning to switch on her computer, Patricia also turns the answer-phone off and puts it into office hours mode.

"The fact is, Palmer took around 50K pounds and

turned it into a few million by working hard and investing wisely. Connor turned his into fast cars and even faster women who helped him to spend his money like water."

"And now he works for his rich brother," Zoe put in with a grimace. "No wonder he was steamed – it's a bitter pill to swallow when you both started out with the same amount of money."

Patricia looks taken aback. "Don't tell me you're feeling sorry for Connor?" Then she seems to catch herself and gives an embarrassed cough. "Well, you'll see for yourself in time."

Her first day is filled with so much information that the end comes all too fast. "Will we be able to work together tomorrow?" she asks Patricia with a tired smile.

"Oh, yes. And don't go home worrying your pretty head about those boys," she warns Zoe warmly. "They usually make it up before long and I've never actually known them to come to blows."

In the lift, Zoe thinks back over the day and wonders where the time went. There are so many aspects to the job that she hadn't thought off. *At least I've got Patricia! Thank the Lord for small mercies.*

After eating the dinner her mother had prepared, Zoe takes herself off for a soak in the bath. Her feet are aching even though she kept her shoes low heeled – she'd done so much walking her arches had arches.

"Oooh, bliss," she moans in pleasure as the perfumed water laps around and over her body. Closing her eyes she allows her mind to drift.

A picture of Palmer Johnson fills her mind and this time her moan is one of secret pleasure.

He is one seriously built man! When Patricia called them 'boys', I could have laughed out loud.

Boys are like Mark and Andrew, the only two boys I've ever been out with. But Palmer and Connor are in a league of their own – and way, way, way out of mine!

Arriving at the office early, Zoe isn't surprised to have beat Patricia in. She wants to have a good look around on her own. If she can remember where things are kept it will be a big help, and she takes out her notebook of code numbers.

"Ok, so that's the fax code, the photocopier and the staff loo," she mutters out loud. Turning on the computer she inputs the password that Patricia had given her and she had written down in her notebook. "Good, we're up and running!"

"Well that's good to hear," Palmer steps out of his office and into hers, "because Patricia went into labour early in the night!"

Zoe almost jumps off her seat, not having realised that

her boss is already in. Then she pales visibly and Palmer becomes concerned.

"She...isn't coming...back?"

"Are you alright? Do you want me to get you some water?" he asks solicitously.

"I think I feel sick!" And she isn't kidding – one day of basic training and she is in at the deep end. Now what is she supposed to do?!

Moving quickly, Palmer puts a hand to the back of her head and pushes her head down into her lap before Zoe can think.

After a second or two of wondering what just happened, Zoe puts a hand up to signal Palmer to let go.

"I'm ok," she tries to tell him, her forehead jammed against her knees, "you can let go now."

"Are you sure?" he asks, still not letting her up. "I think you're supposed to stay down there for a minute or two!"

Bent double, and barely able to breath, Zoe can only gasp for breath and hope he lets go soon.

"Palmer!" A woman's voice gasps the word in panic. "What on earth are you doing to that poor girl?!"

"It's ok, mother – she feels sick, I'm just putting her head in her lap like you used to do for us," he tells her proudly.

Batting him aside, she helps Zoe to sit up and watches as she gulps in air. "Oh, really, you poor thing – you'll be lucky if she doesn't sue you for assault!"

"What? No!" Zoe gasps, "He was just trying...to help."

"And half smothering you in the process!" Dorothy Johnson declares. "Palmer, go and get the girl some water, for heaven's sakes!"

Seeing Palmer dash off, Zoe feels awful for him. "He really was just trying to help, I was just bent over a bit too far," she tries to explain.

"Here now, take a sip of this," Dorothy tells her when Palmer passes her the plastic beaker of water.

"That's great. That's fine, really," she tells them, her cheeks now flushed with embarrassment.

Getting to her feet, Dorothy turns to her son and asks, "What on earth happened? Did you frighten the poor girl?"

"Mother, really – Zoe just had a bit of a panic when she realised that Patricia wouldn't be coming back to work with her today," he explains. "The baby decided to come a couple of weeks early – Bob rang me at 2 in the morning to tell me he'd just taken her into the hospital."

Huffing softly, Dorothy gives a shake of her beautiful head. "Well babies work to their own timetable – we'll just have to muddle through."

"You're staying," he smiles happily.

"Of course, Zoe will have a nervous breakdown if you dump everything onto her at once." Then she turns her attention back to Zoe, who is now breathing a lot easier.

"I used to do all of Palmer's secretarial work when he first started out," she smiles brightly. "I was his father's secretary – that's how we met, so it wasn't anything I couldn't handle," she explains.

"Well, I'd certainly be glad of the help even if it is just for a few hours," Zoe acknowledges gratefully. "Patricia and I went through quite a lot yesterday but I don't think it has all sunk in yet."

"Palmer, do get on, dear," his mother scolds gently. "I thought you were going to the Dersinger site again today – at least, that's what Connor told me this morning."

"I am," Palmer tells her. "I don't usually come to work dressed in my site gear, mother."

"Fine, well, leave us alone and we'll have everything under control before you know it," she tells him, already looking through the post and sorting it into piles.

"Sorry about the bad start," he apologises to Zoe. "I'm sure my mother will have you up and running in no time – I'll try to get back this afternoon."

With that he makes his escape and closes the outer door behind him.

CHAPTER THREE

By mid afternoon, Zoe is starting to feel her feet with the work.

She has a quick mind and works well with Dorothy Johnson, who is a heaven sent organiser.

"Thank you so much for helping me," Zoe tells her at the end of the day. "I would never have managed without you. But did I stop you from doing whatever you had planned for the day," she asks in concern.

"Oh, don't worry about that," Dorothy laughs. "I haven't had so much fun in a long while, and I can go shopping any time."

Pulling on her jacket, Zoe hooks her bag over her shoulder and checks that everything is closed down. Flicking the switch on the answer-phone, she puts it back onto night mode.

The two women walk to the lift together, Palmer having not made it back to the office at all.

"How about coming to us for dinner tonight?" Dorothy invites cordially. "You deserve a good meal and a nice glass of wine after such a harried day."

"You don't have to do that – my mother will be home soon and she usually gets a meal ready," Zoe explains. "But thanks for the offer."

"Bring her with you," Dorothy invites gaily. "We were always having Patricia and Bob over for dinner – I like to get to know those working so closely with my boys."

Again with the 'boys', am I the only one who sees them as men!

Fearing that she might offend their mother, Zoe tentatively agrees. "If I could just give my mother a call, I need to see if she has other plans first."

Not able to use her mobile in the lift, Zoe does so the minute they step out into the car park.

"Hi, mum," Zoe smiles at her mum's cheering reply, "I'm just ringing to see if you're free for dinner this evening? My boss's mum just invited us over – nothing formal," she adds, when Dorothy whispers instructions in her ear.

"You are, ok, I'll come home then we can take a taxi together," Zoe begins, but hesitates when Dorothy vigorously shakes her head.

"Hold on, mum, I think Mrs Johnson has another idea."

"Palmer will be coming, too, he can pick you both up and drop you off again on his way home," Dorothy asserts with a confident smile.

"Ok, mum – I don't know if you heard that…yes, we'll be getting a lift. I'll see you soon," and Zoe rings off while looking at Dorothy with uncertain brown eyes.

"Oh, don't look so worried," Dorothy chuckles. "Palmer won't mind in the least. He's a good boy," she states warmly.

When he stands at her door 2 hours later, Zoe still can't see the boy for the man. "I'm so sorry to put you out like this," she tells him as she waves him into the sitting room and introduces him to her mother. "Mum, this is my boss, Palmer Johnson, and Palmer; this is my mum, Carly Benson."

"Pleased to meet you, Mrs Benson," Palmer gives a small nod of his head to the older woman. "I hope my mother hasn't put any plans out – she can be very impulsive," he apologises with an indulgent smile.

His car is a sleek Jaguar with leather upholstery, and Palmer drives it like an expert. They glide round corners barely registering the movement, and both women are smiling in the back of the car.

"Do you do this for all your employees," Carly Benson asks.

"Mostly," Palmer confirms. "But then we're a small firm and we treat it like a family. I think you'll be meeting Laura from accounting tonight – my mother invited her as well."

Carly and Zoe look at each other, smile and shrug their shoulders. It all sounds normal enough, for them.

By the time they reach Mrs Johnson's house, Zoe is bubbling with excitement. Far from being a shadow child, Zoe has always been gregarious. She loves people and having fun, and at 20 has the energy to throw herself into things full pelt.

Therein lies the problem, as far as her mother is concerned. Carly worries that Zoe is impetuous and far too trusting and will one day get hurt the way she did.

When the car stops and they alight, they find themselves outside a quaint 'chocolate-box' cottage with roses growing around the door.

"How beautiful!" they say together, then laugh at their coordination.

Palmer stands watching the two women, delighted by their easy relationship. He hasn't had much time to get to know his new PA, but from what he's seen so far, he's looking forward to working with her.

"My mother loves it, and my father loves it because

she does," he smiles indulgently then reaches out to put his key in the door and let them in.

"Mum, we're here," he announces loudly, beckoning them to follow as he moves through the house to a surprisingly spacious kitchen.

"Hi," he greets his mother, and bends to kiss her cheek. "Mum, you already know Zoe, but this is Mrs Benson, Zoe's mother."

Reaching a hand out in greeting, Dorothy Johnson's smile is warm and welcoming. "I'm Dorothy; it's so nice that you could come. We like to get to know all of Palmer's employees – we'll be having a barbecue in a couple of weeks where you'll be able to meet them all."

"That's such a lovely thing to do," Carly observes. "And please, call me Carly," she smiles at Palmer and receives an acquiescent nod, then turns back to Dorothy who looks delighted by the introductions.

"Let's go through to the conservatory – it's such a lovely day we have all the doors open and the breeze is so cooling."

It has been a hot summer so far and June has only just begun. The garden is in full bloom, miniature roses of every colour and kind fill the borders, with marigolds in small clusters here and there and a few variegated shrubs adding height to the arrangement.

"You have a lovely garden," Zoe beams at Dorothy, "do you do it all yourself."

Growing tall with pride, Dorothy nods enthusiastically. "I do, actually. I love getting outdoors, planting and weeding. Palmer bought me a greenhouse last year and now I can grow all my own cuttings and seeds."

The greenhouse must be somewhere to the side of the house, Zoe muses, *can't see any sign of it out back.*

"You're a generous son," Carly observes with approval. "It's not always a given in this day and age."

"My mother has always been generous," Palmer replies with a lopsided grin. "With her money, her love and...with her advice."

They all laugh at the implication in his tone, and even his mother joins in.

"I have opinions and I don't mind sharing them," she declares. "But you go your own way no matter what I say, you always have."

"Isn't that how it should be?" Carly smiles at Dorothy. "We raise them with good values, try to guide them along the way, and then have to let them fly off on their own hoping that we've armed them well."

With a frown, Palmer says, "You make it sound like a battle?"

"Isn't it?" Carly replies honestly. "Every day you must

come up against competition – in your work and maybe even in your private life. If you want something more than the other person, you need to strategise and be determined. But even if you win, the loser also has to survive. And maybe one day the loser might be you."

"Mum, really!" Zoe interjects with a laugh. "Don't get all serious on us!"

"No, you're mother is right," Dorothy nods in agreement. "Life can be a test in survival for some, and having the right life-skills can make all the difference."

Palmer and Zoe look at each other, both feeling their parent's serious shroud enveloping them.

"How about a walk in the garden?" Palmer offers, and takes Zoe's hand to lead her outdoors.

Her heart does a leap but Zoe doesn't remove her hand from his and Palmer seems quite content to continue holding it.

"This is so lovely – I can't believe your mother does this all herself," Zoe beams up at her escort.

"It was always a dream of hers – a cottage in the country but not too far away from the town," he explains. "And she's always wanted horses, which she has access to just through here," and he leads the way through a small gate and up a lane at the back of the garden.

"Are these your mother's?" Zoe laughs as she strokes

the velvet muzzle of a very tame horse.

"No, but she visits them most days so she gets to spoil them with apples and the like without the work of keeping them."

"I like to ride," Zoe tells him. "I used to compete in gymkhanas as a child."

"Were you good?"

"Of course!" she asserts, and they both laugh at her confidence. "I just enjoyed the competition, but I did also enjoy collecting the rosettes. I had a cabinet full of them."

"Well, I suppose if a competition is worth entering you should give it your best to try and win it."

"No doubt that's what you've had to do," she observes, her smile more contemplative as she regards the man at her side.

You have a lot of fun in you but there must be a competitive streak in there or you wouldn't be so good at business.

"With the business you mean?" and she nods in reply. "I suppose so. I don't really see it as me against the world, I just try to put in the best bid I can for each job, large or small. And if the competition wins it, I move on to the next."

"No regret, no angst about the loss?" she asks curiously.

"What's the point in that – I might look at what I could have done better but I don't worry over it. Life's too short for regrets," he laughs, and now she can see the boy inside the man.

CHAPTER FOUR

Back in the office the next day, Zoe ploughs into the work with real enthusiasm.

She is still finding her feet, but Palmer is patient with her and is out of the office for most of the day anyway.

When she opens the post, Zoe reads the contents briefly to see what action might be needed and gets a good idea of the work that is tendered for by Johnson Construction.

"Wow!" Zoe exclaims, having opened a follow up to a tender of £1.25 million for a small project on the outskirts of Birmingham.

When she has sorted the post, Zoe has various piles on her desk and takes the appropriate piles to accounting.

"Hi, Laura," Zoe greets the young woman she had met just last night at the cottage. "Did you meet up with

Kenny after dinner last night?"

The girls had gotten on really well the night before and had discussed the men in their lives, or the lack of in Zoe's case.

"The jerk stood me up," Laura frowns. "But he won't do it again – I dumped his arse and told him not to bother calling me again!"

"You did? But you sounded quite fond of him when we spoke last night."

"He's alright – when he has his thinking head on," Laura explains. "But he gets so wrapped up in his work he forgets everything, including me. I've had enough of coming second to his damned research!"

"What kind of research does he do?" Zoe wonders.

"All kinds – he runs a business that offers to find out whatever the client needs," Laura frowns. "I don't really understand it – but he's either at the city library or on his damned computer and he just forgets about everything once he gets started on a project."

"I've never heard of that kind of business before – but I suppose people always need information about something," Zoe smiles brightly.

"How about a night out, just us girls?" Laura asks. "I could do with some fun, and it is Friday so it won't matter if we're out late."

"That's a great idea, we'll discuss it over lunch," Zoe suggests. "I've still got loads of post to sort through. I'd better get back to it."

By 4 o'clock, Zoe has typed up most of the new tenders, done all of the filing and is feeling quite pleased with herself.

When Palmer arrives she tries not to gush – but it's difficult, he makes her stomach flip and knot all at the same time.

"Looks like you're getting the hang of things," Palmer smiles, looking through the typed up tenders that Zoe has put on his desk for checking and signing.

"Your mother helped enormously," she tells him. "I wouldn't have known where to start and we managed to get caught up on most things. It made starting today that much easier," Zoe grins brightly, feeling her cheeks pink.

Why do I have to blather on when I'm nervous? It makes me sound like an imbecile!

"Good to know," Palmer returns her smile, and then stands thumbing through the small pile of tenders. "These are fine; can you get them in the post tonight?"

"No problem," she tells him. "There's a post box on the way home that has a late pick up."

"Are you enjoying the work?" Palmer asks after signing the tenders.

"Yes, thank you. Do I ever get to go on-site?" she asks enthusiastically.

Palmer is taken aback by her question. *Hmm, Patricia was never interested, but it might be alright...if we can find site boots small enough and a safety hat that fits?*

"I'll have a think about it over the weekend," he tells her. "What size shoes do you take?"

Her eyebrows shoot up, but Zoe tells him, "I'm a size 4, why?"

"I need to get you some site boots," and he stands frowning down at her tiny feet. "I'm not sure that they come in that size...you have really small feet!"

Blushing, Zoe moves them uncomfortably. "Sorry."

"Not to worry, I'm sure we'll come up with something." Handing Zoe the signed tenders, Palmer perches on the edge of his desk as he's still in his work clothes. "Got any plans for the weekend?"

Smiling happily now, Zoe tells him of hers and Laura's plans for a night out. "She just broke up with her boyfriend, Kenny, so I think she just wants to party a bit."

"Going anywhere nice?"

"I've got no idea – we didn't really get down to the nitty-gritty," Zoe laughs. "I suppose we'll just meet up somewhere and decide from there."

"Well, be careful," Palmer advises, not really knowing

why he should care what his new PA does in her own time. "There are some dodgy areas in the city centre. You might do better to stick to the outskirts."

"Thanks, we will," she tells him, then returns to her office.

Having mailed the post on the way home, Zoe pulls into the drive and parks her car.

Almost skipping into the house, Zoe greets her mother and tells her about the planned night out.

"You'll need to eat a good meal before you go out," Carly advises sagely.

"Ok, mum, but I'm going up to have a shower first." And Zoe runs up the stairs with an energy only enjoyed by the young.

It's been a while since Zoe has had a girl's night out. She finished with her own boyfriend about four months ago and hasn't felt much like going out since.

Not that it had been an acrimonious split, she just wanted to get her course work finished and put the time in to get the best possible grades.

As was her habit, if something was worth doing, Zoe did it the best she could.

Drying and straightening her long auburn hair, Zoe hums to herself and jigs about on the spot. She really is in the mood for a dance.

Pulling on her strappy blue sateen mini dress with matching strappy heeled shoes, Zoe does a twirl in front of the mirror and decides that a touch of eye-makeup should finish the look off nicely.

"You look lovely," Carly smiles at her daughter, pleased that she is getting out again.

"I'm not really sure where we're going," Zoe tells her mother. "Laura suggested meeting outside work – it's fairly central and easy to get to by bus."

"Good idea, but be careful of the city centre, Zoe," her mother cautions. "Those bigger nightclubs sometimes attract trouble."

"Don't worry, mum, we were only planning to go to a bar with a dance-floor. Nothing too outrageous," she giggles at her mother's worrywarting.

A couple of hours later Zoe and Laura walk into the Penny-farthing bar. It is a sizeable bar with a good sized dance-floor and an upstairs area for easy seating with lots of low tables and two-seater settees.

Just an hour later and the place is heaving. The music is loud and just right for dancing which pleases Zoe and Laura.

"Hey, there's Connor, I didn't know he came here!" Laura shouts to Zoe over the music. "Hey, Connor," Laura waves over to the tall young man who is attracting lots of female attention.

Zoe isn't as sure about inviting Connor over as Laura seems to be, but doesn't have a choice in the matter.

"Well, well, if it isn't our own Laura and Zoe – what are you two doing here?" Connor asks with a sexy smirk.

Laura appears to drink him in, but Zoe doesn't like the way he is looking at her.

"We're celebrating my single status," Laura announces with a lift of her chin.

"Then we need some drinks, let's go upstairs for a bit. It's deafening down here," Connor suggests and moves off assuming they will follow.

Laura is dead keen and grabs Zoe's arm when she lags behind.

Connor's friends have bagged a couple of settee's overlooking the downstairs dance-floor and are watching the activity below. Laura marches straight up to the bar and stands at Connor's side.

"What are you drinking?" he turns and smiles down at Laura, then turns his head further to include Zoe in his offer.

"Just tonic water for me," Zoe tells him, and gets a lifted eyebrow in reply.

"Put a gin in that for me," Laura laughs, and without Zoe realising he orders two.

Carrying a tray with three pints of beer and the two

gin and tonics, Connor guides them over to the table where his friends are already sat.

"Gary, Michael, this is Laura and Zoe," he introduces. "They work for my brother."

"Like you," Gary laughs, winding Connor up.

"Yeah, funny guy," Connor scowls at the other men, then reaches out to pull Laura down beside him.

She giggles, but settles into him happily enough.

Zoe sits on a stool between the two settees, glad that she wasn't the one sitting next to Connor.

After a couple more drinks Laura is relaxing into Connor a little too much for Zoe's liking. She has made the first drink he bought her last, it tastes strange and she isn't sure that he isn't trying to get them drunk.

She is just thinking to drag Laura up and onto the dance-floor when Connor moves in for a kiss. Laura doesn't protest and the kiss becomes heated. Then Connor opens his eyes and stares at Zoe while kissing Laura outrageously.

His behaviour shocks Zoe but she can't drag her eyes away from his.

"Hey," Laura protests when Zoe grabs her hand and pulls her up. "Where are we going?"

"Nowhere!" Connor scowls up at Zoe, but she manages to pull Laura out of his reach.

"We're going on the dance-floor, that's what we came here for after-all," Zoe tells Laura as she drags her to the stairs.

"But..." Laura doesn't get to finish her protest as she has to hold onto the handrail and concentrate on not falling down the spiral staircase after Zoe.

"Do you really like that creep?" Zoe asks when they finally make it to the dance-floor. "I mean, you only just broke up with Kenny – who knows, you might get back together?"

"I think Connor's great," Laura smiles broadly. "And he can kiss better than any boy I've ever met!"

Zoe frowns; *Perhaps you wouldn't think that if I told you what he did. But then, what can I say, he looked at me all the while he was kissing you?*

They dance and Zoe eventually forgets all about Connor and his friends. For the most part they dance together but occasionally accept a dance with casual guys who just want some fun.

It isn't until they are getting ready to leave that Connor makes his presence known again.

"How about a lift, gorgeous?" he whispers into Laura's ear and makes her laugh.

Much to Zoe's disappointment, she watches Laura nod and lean in for a kiss. Again, Zoe finds herself looking into Connor's eyes while he kisses her new friend. She doesn't like the look in them and decides to warn Laura about him at the first opportunity.

Connor drops his mates off first, both of them the worse for wear, and then he drops off Laura.

"Couldn't you drop me off first," Zoe pleads, not wanting to find herself alone with Connor.

"Yeah," Laura agrees, "then I can give you a proper kiss goodnight."

But Connor is already pulling into Laura's street. "You live nearest and we're here now," Connor argues pleasantly.

When he swings the car into her parent's drive, Laura sulks prettily. "You could have put yourself out just a little!"

"Maybe next time," he purrs, and makes Zoe's flesh crawl.

Then she has a brainwave, or more a flash of self-preservation. "No problem, I'll come in with you anyway," Zoe proclaims, and exits the car before anyone can protest.

When she looks back at Laura still sitting in the front passenger seat, she can see Connor looking none too pleased over her shoulder.

Well you can get the hump, I don't care. There is no way I'm going to be on my own with you tonight, or any other night!

CHAPTER FIVE

The office is busy when she arrives at work on Monday. Palmer is discussing a job with Connor and a couple of other men.

Keeping herself out of the way, Zoe gets on with sorting the post and answering the telephone.

When Palmer finally comes through to talk to her, Zoe tries to keep her head down and look extremely busy.

"Hi, Zoe, I managed to get you some boots," Palmer declares happily. "Fancy a visit to the site today?"

"Well, there's a lot of post and I've got several tenders to type up and...and..." she tails off at Connors look of derision over his brother's shoulder.

"I thought you were keen to see what it is we do?" Palmer asks, sounding disappointed and a little confused.

"I'd love to," Zoe smiles up at him, then sweeps a hand over the piles of post on her desk, "but wouldn't you rather I get this sorted?"

Shaking his head, Palmer laughs, "That's ongoing — time to see what this company is really all about!"

"Ok," Zoe tries to return his smile, but feels it tremor when she catches Connor's eye.

Connor and the other two men take one firm's van and Palmer and Zoe take another.

"How did your night out with Laura go?" he asks chattily. "I saw Laura earlier and she didn't look the worse for wear."

"Well, we've had a couple of days to get over it," Zoe jokes, then falters when he frowns.

"You got drunk?" Palmer asks.

"No, but we were out late and Connor did buy us a couple of drinks," she adds, not sure why she is nervous about telling him that.

"Connor was with you? I didn't realise you were all going out together." Palmer doesn't sound angry, but Zoe just knows that he isn't happy about it.

"No, we didn't," she tells him quickly. "He came into the bar later and then offered to buy us a drink. I think he and Laura hit it off though."

Palmer seems to relax a little after that, though he still isn't pleased about something.

"You think Connor made a pass at her?" he asks lightly.

Why do I get the feeling he's really making a move on you? Laura isn't his type and Connor likes nothing more than having something he knows I want. He would have seen that at dinner the other night – I didn't exactly hide it! Damn it!

"They did...kind of...hit it off," she repeats, not wanting to say that they had been snogging like they needed a room!

"Ok. I suppose Laura is old enough to take care of herself," Palmer concedes.

"And I'm not?" Zoe asks, stung.

"I didn't say that," Palmer frowns across at her.

But they don't get to talk anymore as he pulls the van onto the building site.

"Just take notes and stay right beside me," Palmer tells Zoe, making sure that her hard hat is fitted properly. "I don't have time to make an impromptu visit to the hospital!"

Palmer tells Connor what he wants doing and sends him off to supervise the other men. He doesn't look happy about it when he flashes a look at Zoe before moving off. But Palmer barely notices.

He continues talking with the architect, and Zoe takes notes as they walk around the site.

"You know," Terry Fielding, the architect, stops and

looks at Palmer, "if you're really interested in tendering for the Rodriguez Hotel project, you're going to need to fly out there."

Zoe continues to scribble notes on her pad, including the name of the hotel, and remembers reading a letter about the proposed project.

It's in Italy; maybe Palmer will want an assistant? Oh, I hope so.

Connor is being bullish – Zoe can hear him ordering men about but when she watches, doesn't see him doing much hard labour himself.

Then she notices Palmer watching him and stands back when he moves across to talk to his brother.

She doesn't have to hear what he says; Zoe can see the heat in Connor's cheeks and the livid look in his eyes as he watches his brother cross back to her side.

"Come on," Palmer snaps out, "let's get back to the office."

For the rest of the morning and part of the afternoon, Palmer stays in his office leaving her to get on with her work.

She knows when he's on the office phone as it lights up on hers. When it rings it makes her jump and it's Palmer asking her to come through.

Taking her notepad and pencil, Zoe takes a seat

opposite Palmer and waits nervously for him to start dictation.

But he doesn't. Palmer considers her for a moment or two, not saying anything at all. Then he sits forward and puts both forearms on the desk in front of him.

"I've decided to tender for the Rodriguez Hotel project," he tells her with a frown. "It will mean being in Italy for around a week and there's a second project in Malaga that I might take a look at, at the same time."

Zoe hasn't written a thing on her notepad, but she is watching him and taking in every word.

"Ok, do you need me to book the flights and accommodation?" she asks, as this would normally fall under her remit.

"Do you have a current passport?" Palmer asks instead of answering her question, and when she nods he simply says, "Good! Cancel all my appointments for next week – we'll fly out on Monday and be back by Friday, if all goes to plan."

"Do you want me to try to move any of next week's appointments into this week?" Zoe asks, now taking notes and on full alert.

"Yes, fit Jostle and Colbert in and get hold of Craig Stanley – he won't be best pleased to be pulled off the Hockley Brook project but I want him running the Aston site from now on. Connor isn't pulling his weight; Craig will make sure that he does!"

Before she leaves, Zoe glances at his desk and sees no sign of Palmer having eaten anything.

"Mr Johnson...I bought extra sandwiches at lunch time; they're corned beef," she tells him. "Can I get them for you?"

Sitting back in his chair, he looks up and smiles. "That's very considerate, thank you," he tells her. "Though, I don't expect you to get my lunch on a regular basis."

Her smile widening, Zoe goes off to the staff kitchen to fetch the sandwiches and puts them on a small plate and makes a cup of black coffee to go with them.

"Here you go," Zoe smiles, placing the meal and drink in front of her boss.

When she turns to leave, Palmer stops her, "Zoe...what's with the Mr Johnson title – we were on first name terms before our visit to the building site?"

Blushing, Zoe realises that she had been annoyed with him and hadn't even realised that she had used his formal title. "I'm sorry, I know you asked me to call you Palmer, but sometimes I just forget."

"Don't let it happen again," he tells her, trying to keep a straight face, but when her eyes go round and large he takes pity and smiles at her.

"Oh! Oh, no sir, I mean, Palmer," she stammers and retreats hastily back into her own little sanctuary.

Taking a sip of the coffee she has made for herself, Zoe gets on to rearranging Palmers diary and also gets in touch with Craig Stanley.

"Yes, Mr Stanley, I'll let Mr Johnson know!"

"Chewed your ear off a bit, didn't he?" Palmer chuckles, watching her from the doorway between their offices.

"He...Mr Stanley wasn't happy and is coming in this evening to have words," she tells Palmer, emphasising the last two words as Craig Stanley had done.

Laughing out loud now, Palmer finishes the coffee he's holding then puts the empty mug on Zoe's desk. "Thanks for that, and the sandwiches were great too."

She didn't see Palmer again until almost finishing time. Craig Stanley marched into her office dressed in site gear and looking amazingly sexy considering he was dressed in ripped jeans and a vest top that had long seen better days.

"Is he in?" Craig barks out the minute he enters her office.

"I...who exactly are you?" Zoe asks nervously, then thinks about the call she had placed to the Hockley Brook site earlier. "Are you..."

"That's alright," Palmer tells her from their shared doorway. "Craig, get in here and stop frightening my secretary! She isn't used to you rough types yet!"

Standing, Zoe tries to look all of her 5 feet 5 inches and holds her head up proudly, "Would you like coffee bringing in?" she asks bravely.

"Yes!" Craig barks out in his gravelly voice.

"No!" Palmer countermands sharply. "We can get it ourselves – you get off. I'll see you in the morning."

With that the office door closes and Zoe is left feeling confused.

Then she hears raised voices, Craig's first and then Palmers. Collecting her bag, Zoe makes her way to the lift and decides that she should make the most of an early finish.

Driving into town, she decides to do a bit of shopping. If she's going to be going to Italy and Malaga with her boss then she doesn't want to show him up.

Trying on a peach coloured Linen suit, Zoe looks at herself in the mirror and decides that it compliments her honeyed skin tone and auburn hair nicely.

"It emphasises those beautiful brown eyes," the shop assistant tells her persuasively, and Zoe can't resist.

"Ok, I'll take that and the duck-egg blue suit," she tells the assistant. "And, maybe I will look at the bikinis – I know it's a business trip, but you never know..."

"And it pays to be prepared," the assistant cajoles, thinking of her sales target.

By the time she gets home, Zoe has bought three new summer weight suits and two bikinis.

"What's all the shopping?" Carly Benson asks her daughter when Zoe walks in the door clutching three shopping bags.

Beaming with excitement, Zoe shows her the suits but keeps the bikinis hidden.

"Palmer needs to go to Italy and maybe Malaga to assess jobs that he may want to tender for," Zoe bubbles out enthusiastically.

"And he's asked you to go with him?" her mother asks sceptically.

"I'm his PA, mother," Zoe states indignantly.

"Just make sure that is all you are!" Carly exclaims, and turns to go back into the kitchen to finish cooking their evening meal.

Isn't that what I was, before I became Douglas Benson's bit-on-the-side! Men are all the same – they see a vulnerable young woman and just have to take advantage! Well I won't have it...not for Zoe!

The silence is palpable over the dinner table. Zoe has no idea what she's done wrong and Carly can't help projecting her own past onto Zoe's future.

This trip to Italy could be a ruse, a way of tempting a young woman into bed and into a relationship that she isn't yet ready to handle! Any more than I was at her age, Carly remembers soberly.

CHAPTER SIX

With her mother's warnings ringing in her ears, Zoe opens the front door to Palmer and he takes her suitcase to his car.

"Please, mum," Zoe hugs and gives her mother a kiss, "if you're ever going to trust me now is when I need it – ok?"

"Ok," Carly tells her, returning the hug with all her heart. "Go to work, but have fun on your time off."

The drive to the airport isn't a long one. And, as they are setting off on a very early flight, there isn't much traffic about.

"Was your mum really ok about you making this trip?" Palmer asks solicitously.

"You know what mum's can be," Zoe smiles and cringes all at once. "But she sees this job as a good opportunity for me – just as I do."

Keeping his eyes on the road, Palmer considers this for a while.

"Where do you see yourself in five years time?" he asks, a question that Patricia, as one of the interviewing panel, had asked before.

Zoe considers, then tells him more or less what she had before. Only now, she can be more expansive about it.

"Your company is growing – it's big now, but you obviously have expansion plans," she tells him. "I want to be a part of that. I'd like to make my job as involved in what you do as you will allow me. Like helping to source materials – finding more competitive prices and offering a wider variety of finishes to the client.

"Like, I was looking at some tiles on the internet...," and now Zoe has turned in her seat to better look at Palmer, "...we offer a really good quality floor tile in a small variety of colour-ways and styles – there's a supplier in Spain that can do them at 2/3rds the price including shipping, and maybe even less if we order larger quantities from him. And he's willing to supply a catalogue with lots of colour-ways and styles for us to show our clients.

"And he isn't the only one," she continues excitedly. "Roof tiles! There are a couple of suppliers in Italy that already ship to this country and would be happy to offer competitive rates for reasonably large orders. And their initial quotes are excellent!"

Chuckling at her unbridled enthusiasm, Palmer pulls into the airport's long-term parking and turns off the engine. "You've really given this some thought," he turns in his seat and gives her an admiring smile. "So, you've found the time to explore these other markets as well as keep up with the everyday work?"

"Yes, now that I'm starting to feel the rhythm of the work, I'm sure I could do more on the sourcing side of things," she offers eagerly.

"So, your job is so boring that you go trolling the internet in your spare time?" Palmer frowns with pursed lips.

"No! Oh, no!" Zoe protests quickly. "I just saw some of the supplier's bills and wondered if I could find better prices," Zoe's large brown eyes have rounded and she looks very unsure.

"Don't look so worried," Palmer laughs, "I'm just kidding. If you can find the time to do it, then by all means source me some cheaper materials – just don't compromise on the quality. Our reputation has taken a long while to build, it can be lost overnight if we aren't careful."

Walking into the terminal, Palmer managing to carry her suitcase as well as his own, they check-in and sit in business class awaiting their flight.

Over a cup of coffee, Palmer continues their discussion. "So, you see yourself still being with us in five years?"

Zoe blushes, realising that she never did properly answer his question. "I'd like to think so. I'd just like to expand the role a little."

Considering this, Palmer stirs his coffee then takes a sip. "You enjoyed getting out on site, I take it?"

"I did. I really did," Zoe enthuses. "Attending site meetings would be an ideal way of getting to know the ins and outs of the business. As well as building up relationships with clients. They can feel more confident in contacting me instead of always calling you," she offers.

"And that would be a very good thing," Palmer reflects, the idea of getting a few of them off his back making Zoe's idea sound very enticing.

"Let's see how you do with the Rodriguez family — they are very traditional, apparently, so may not find dealing with a woman to their taste," and Palmer smiles as her chin lifts.

"As you say, let's just see how I do."

The flight is short and uneventful, and Zoe is raring to

go when they step out of the airport. She has arranged a hire car for the week and they pick that up and drive straight to the hotel site in Sorrento.

It is a run-down building that has been in the family for generations. Tucked away on the coastline, it has only recently been earmarked for extensive renovation.

The Rodriguez family know it will not be able to compete with the larger resort hotels, but wants to offer a more individual and personal service for the more discerning traveller.

Retrieving the plans from his suitcase, Palmer guides Zoe into the hotel's lobby and he spreads them out to take a look and get his bearings.

Then a man hurries over to meet them. "I am Alonzo Abbatelli," the stunning looking man declares, "how may I help you?" Then he looks down at the plans that Palmer has laid out and realises who they are. "Ah, your Mr Fielding said you would be arriving sometime today – was your trip comfortable?"

His eyes flick to Palmer as he asks the question, but they rest on Zoe as he smiles and bows his head in greeting.

Watching Zoe melt under the Italian's gaze, Palmer finds himself becoming instantly annoyed.

"Perhaps we could just wander around, look at the

plans and get a feel for the place," Palmer suggests brusquely. So brusquely that Zoe flashes him a questioning frown.

"No, no, it would be my pleasure to escort you," Alonzo smiles radiantly, and causes Zoe's heart to do a complete summersault. "I am the site manager; I must ensure your safety."

On saying that, he crosses the room and comes back with two hard hats and takes the time to fit Zoe's himself.

"It is a shame to cover such beautiful hair," he tells her. "But we must keep you safe at all costs."

When his hand brushes her hair and then her cheek, Zoe feels herself blush and he lets out a low sexy chuckle.

The tour takes much longer than Palmer would have liked. The Italian 'Bonzo' as he has taken to calling him in his head, has manipulated Zoe the whole time, paying him lip service only.

By the time they leave, Palmer's blood is heating up right along with the Italian temperature, and it promises to be a very hot day.

"You didn't say you spoke Italian," he grouches when they get back in the rental car.

"I barely do," Zoe laughs. "But Alonzo was kind enough to take his time and speak in very basic terms."

"Really! How very obliging of him," Palmer frowns, driving with studious care.

Zoe isn't sure, but Palmer doesn't look very happy.

What did I do? I got the man on side – he said he'd be happy to deal with me about the tender. What more does Palmer want?

When they pull up outside of their hotel, Palmer rounds the car and takes out their suitcases then ushers Zoe inside.

At check-in, he deals quickly with the formalities then takes both keys and moves across to a small lift.

"Let's just get settled in then we can discuss the tender – if I decide to tender at all," he adds, surprising Zoe into maintaining her silence.

Their rooms are opposite each other, and Palmer sees Zoe into hers before leaving her to go to his.

Alone, she wanders out to the small wrought iron balcony and looks out over the Mediterranean Sea.

I thought Palmer would be pleased that I can speak a little Italian. I even brushed up on it before we came. But he looked annoyed, if not down-right angry most of the time...what the heck did I do wrong?!

Palmer flips his suitcase onto the bed and unzips it roughly. Then, deciding he can't be bothered to unpack for the sake of two days, he drops it onto the floor and kicks it under the bed.

Damn it! I need a shower and some food, and a damn

big glass of wine to wash away the nasty taste the Italian stallion has left in my mouth. Damned grease-ball! Smooth and slick and Zoe fell for it like she was a love-struck teenager!

Dressed and ready to go down to lunch, Zoe tries not to worry about what she might have done wrong at the Rodriguez Hotel site. She's already gone over the morning with a fine toothed comb and can't come up with anything that could have put Palmer in such a mood.

I'll just have to play it by ear and hope he's feeling more amenable.

Crossing the landing, she tentatively knocks on his door and waits for Palmer to answer. But when he does Zoe can only stare open mouthed.

Dressed, or undressed, in just a towel slung low over his hips and another in his hands drying off his hair, Palmer just says, "Yes," without realising who is at his door.

"I...I..." With her mouth opening and closing like a guppy's, Zoe can't stop staring at Palmer's exquisite body.

"Christ! Come on in – I took longer than I realised in the shower," he tells her, turning back into his room and walking into the bathroom. "I won't be a minute," he calls out, "just make yourself at home."

When he emerges, Palmer is dressed in a short-sleeved white cotton shirt and comfortable brown corduroy trousers.

Watching him pad barefoot across the room, Zoe doubts she has seen anyone as sexy as Palmer looks right now. She isn't very experienced with men, but she knows a great body when she sees one – and she most definitely had seen one when he'd opened the door to her.

Dragging her mind out of the gutter, Zoe tries for a professional air.

"Do you really doubt that you'll put in a tender for the hotel work?" she asks quietly.

"I'm just not sure it's for us," Palmer shrugs. "But I'll take a closer look at the plans and maybe pay the site another visit before we leave."

"Oh good," Zoe smiles brightly, "maybe I'll get to use my Italian again!"

Then, for no reason that Zoe can see, Palmer frowns and his reply is just a low growl.

With his socks and shoes now pulled on, Palmer turns to Zoe.

"Let's just get some lunch then we'll see what's what."

They walk up to the main Piazza Tasso where lots of scooters zip in and out of traffic. Taking her hand, Palmer guides Zoe through the melee of tourists and locals and up a small alley to a lovely ristorante.

They are seated next to the windows with a breath-taking view of the Mediterranean rolling in on the shore below them.

"You seem to know this place," Zoe observes, and is pleased to see that Palmer appears brighter now.

"This was one of the first places I came to as a teenager going abroad without my parents for the first time," he tells her with a gleam in his blue eyes.

"Hmm, I'm thinking 'watch out Italy'," she grins mischievously. "I'll bet you were a lad about town when you were a teenager."

Laughing, Palmer enjoys this lighter side of Zoe and encourages the flow of conversation away from work.

As they peruse the menu, he asks, "Didn't you go a little wild on your first holiday without your parents?"

"I don't know that I'd call it 'wild' but I certainly let my hair down a little more," she giggles delightfully.

Their conversation is easy and playful, and the meal is superb.

"Oh my goodness – I'm going to put on a lot of weight if the food is as good as this the whole trip!" Zoe sits back with a hand on her well filled stomach.

"You can afford it," Palmer tells her appreciatively. "I don't suppose you thought to pack any swimwear?

Blushing, Zoe nods, "As a matter of fact, I did. It was

just on the off-chance that we got a bit of free time," she explains hurriedly.

"Great, let's walk back to the hotel and collect it then we can go down to the Marina Grande for a swim."

Having changed into her bikini and pulled a loose fitting tunic over the top, Zoe waits on the landing between their rooms for Palmer to emerge.

When he does, Zoe frowns at his unchanged appearance and the empty towel slung over his shoulder.

"I put them on underneath," he smiles and takes her hand. "Here, put this in with yours," he tells her, handing Zoe the towel to stow in her beach-bag. "I'm not sure how the hotel would feel about us taking their towels to the beach."

<u>CHAPTER SEVEN</u>

The beach isn't quite what Zoe has been expecting. It isn't miles of soft golden sand but they can lay a towel down and sunbathe on it all-the-same.

"Are you up for a swim?" Palmer asks, already stripping off his shirt and trousers in readiness.

Grinning and nodding, Zoe kicks off her sandals and pulls her tunic over her head then runs for the water before Palmer has even finished.

"Hey, that's cheating," he calls after her, but catches up fast.

They enter the sea at the same time, both striking out with confidence into the soft waves.

Zoe has always been a strong swimmer and keeps up with him well, though she has a sneaking feeling that Palmer is holding back.

When they turn to head back she finds out just how much he was holding back.

"Come on slow coach," he teases once they enter shallow water, and he strikes out for the beach leaving her in his wake.

"Show off," Zoe rolls her eyes when she catches up to him at the beach then splashes a hand in the water and aims it at him.

In reaction, Palmer lifts her by the knees and throws her back in the water then watches her laugh and thrash to find her feet again.

Once he sees that she is safe, Palmer turns to head back to their towels, then feels her jump on his back almost knocking him off balance.

"Just for that, you can carry me back to the towels; the stones hurt my feet anyway." She laughs as he hitches her up and holds her legs around him more firmly.

The afternoon sun is hot and dries their swimwear in no time. Putting on sun-lotion, Zoe offers the bottle to Palmer meaning for him to put some on himself, but he makes a circling movement with his finger for her to turn around.

"No matter how you try, you can never apply sun-lotion to your own back," he tells her, his firm hand now travelling over her back not missing a spot.

Her breathing is definitely more ragged by the time he has finished and Zoe can only hope that Palmer hasn't noticed.

"Ok, your turn," Zoe grins, holding the lotion bottle at the ready.

When her smaller hands travel over his back, she feels every hard muscle and dip and hollow. Like Palmer, she doesn't miss a spot. And by the time they turn to look at each other again they both look hotter than ever!

Lying back on her towel, Zoe closes her eyes and just hopes her cheeks aren't as red as they feel.

For an hour, they do nothing but sunbathe enjoying a little banter and renewing their lotion more often than is strictly necessary.

"You don't want to burn," Palmer warns when she turns onto her stomach and he lathers her in lotion again.

But Zoe doesn't protest, even when he strokes down the backs of her legs with large firm hands.

"That feels so relaxing," she purrs, as he uses both hands to massage her back.

"Anything to oblige," then he flicks open the catch on her top and bares her entire back. "You don't want lines," Palmer tells her when she gasps, and his hands go back to massaging her skin.

She must have nodded off, because the next thing Zoe

knows is when Palmer gives her a poke in the ribs while calling her name.

Completely forgetting that her top is undone, Zoe rolls over and sits up.

"That's...quite a look," Palmer tells her, his eyes out on stalks for a moment. Then he quickly rolls off his own towel and drapes it about her shoulders, shielding her nakedness from those around them.

Trying to cover her embarrassment, Zoe lifts her chin and tells him, "I've sunbathed topless before." But doesn't bother to add that it was in the sole company of other women.

"Well, whatever, I'm sorry about that. I should have reminded you that the catch was still undone!" *But I can't for the life of me regret my mistake. You are one curvy woman and I love having my hands on you!*

His eyes must have shown some of what he was feeling as Zoe blushes deeper under his gaze.

"We'd better get back to work," Palmer stands and offers Zoe a hand. "Would you like me to hold that while you pull your tunic on?"

He isn't trying to make her uncomfortable, but she feels it anyway.

Turning the gap of the towel to her back, Zoe turns so that Palmer can hold it closed while she reaches down to pick up her tunic and then pull it on.

When she is decent again, Zoe moves away from Palmer's close proximity to allow herself to breathe again. The man takes all her oxygen when he stands too close, she is almost panting by the time she has the beach-bag packed and her sandals back on.

The walk back to their hotel is a long, slow trek up lots of steps. There really hadn't seemed to be so many on the way down!

But finally, they step back into the air-conditioned reception and walk over to the lift. Neither of them is up for walking up the stairs, even if they are only on the third floor.

"Take a couple of hours down," Palmer tells her as they stand between their rooms, "you look like you could use some rest."

At any other time her pride might have kicked in, but right now he was more right than he knew.

"Thank you, I will. Are you going to get some rest?" she asks, hoping that he will so that she doesn't feel so guilty.

"I might," he smiles noncommittally. "I'll give you a knock when I'm ready to go through the plans."

"So, you're going to tender?" she asks, wondering if he's changed his mind.

"Not sure yet, but we'll take a look and then I'll decide."

In her room, Zoe strips off and dives under a lukewarm shower. It's so hot and her hair feels sticky, but the running water soon washes away the clammy feeling and refreshed and clean, she vigorously towels herself dry.

Not bothering to put any clothes on, Zoe lays on top of the bed with the windows open and falls asleep with a wonderful breeze wafting over her.

At first her dreams are playful; Palmer tossing her backwards into the sea, or joking with her as they walk around the Rodriguez Hotel, or just laughing together as they walk along streets and gaze through shop windows.

But they take a more sinister tone when voices become raised. Alonzo showing her into various rooms at the hotel has trapped her in one of them and is trying to kiss her. No matter how she tries to ward him off, he is insistent that it is what she really wants.

Then he changes into Connor – his eyes watching her the way they had when he'd been kissing Laura. His mouth is closing in on hers and Zoe is trapped. Like a butterfly that can't turn away from a light that is luring it to its death, Zoe can only watch as his face draws nearer.

Knocking at her hotel room door wakes Zoe from a dream that is fast becoming a nightmare.

Pulling on the bathrobe that the hotel has kindly supplied, Zoe crosses to answer the door.

Palmer stands tall and bright-eyed in her doorway. "You don't look ready for a planning meeting," he smiles indulgently.

"Sorry," Zoe yawns, then returns his smile. "I had a shower then flaked out on the bed. I didn't wake up until you just knocked, sorry."

"Stop apologising. I've got everything set out in my room, just come in when you're ready."

Lordy, Lordy, how does he look good enough to eat in this heat? And I'll bet he didn't have a sleep!

Pulling on a casual but smart white blouse and calf length skirt, Zoe crosses to Palmer's room and knocks before opening the door.

Sure enough, the hotel plans are spread out across his bed and some on the small table nearby. Either he had been lucky enough to get two chairs in his room, or Palmer had asked them for another.

He is sitting on one at the small table and there is a spare seat for her. Crossing to it, Zoe sits and looks at the plans that Palmer is deep in thought over.

"From a practical point of view I'd like to knock this building down and start again," he tells her as she leans over to see what he is looking at.

When she lets out a small gasp, Palmer turns to smile at her. "Not that I would seriously consider doing that.

The old place has real character — it's impossible to replace that once it's gone."

"So, what's the alternative?" she frowns up at him.

"There's no doubt in my mind that the old place will fall down around the Rodriguez's ears if it isn't shored up properly, and soon. But it isn't irreparable," he concedes, much to Zoe's delight.

She had fallen in love with the hotel's original character. It might be falling to pieces now, but once it had been elegant and regal and she could almost wish that she had been alive in its hay-day to witness this first hand.

"You could do something incredible with this place," she tells Palmer, holding the plans for the dining room.

When he leans across her to see better, Zoe feels her heart trip and speed up alarmingly.

He turns to look at her; Zoe lets out a small moan without realising and Palmer feels it at his core.

His blue eyes hold a storm in them as he looks into the melting chocolate of hers. The heat that has sprung up between them is suddenly all consuming and neither of them have the clarity of mind to break away.

Before either of them can think, Zoe drops the plans unnoticed to the floor and her arms wind about his neck, pulling his lips to hers.

He doesn't need any more encouragement than her obvious desire – Palmer feels it too and is only too willing to give in to it.

The kiss is an explosion of passion, a meeting of mouths that expresses the meeting of minds and hearts and souls.

How can so much be conveyed in a kiss? How can this physical act be so simple yet so intimate, so compelling?

When his hands reach down to cup her full round breast, Zoe only strains forward to offer him more.

When her head falls back to expose her throat, Palmer's lips trail down to taste the heat of her skin and feel the pulse jump as his tongue and teeth nip and tease.

Their minds are flying, their hunger only just beginning to make itself known, when a knock at the door brings them struggling back to reality and some semblance of sanity.

"No," the single word is strangled from Zoe's throat when her arms realise they are empty and the heat of him is gone.

"Thank you," she hears Palmer say to someone, and watches him open the door to admit someone with a tray of tea and sandwiches.

The door closes and they are alone again, staring at each other not quite knowing what to do.

"Would you like some tea?" Palmer asks tentatively. "I ordered it earlier thinking we might need something around now."

But Zoe can only shake her head; she doesn't trust her voice not to betray her disappointment.

This is probably a good thing. We just got carried away...maybe we would have regretted going any further. And maybe Palmer already regrets crossing the line with me? Oh damn my raging hormones!

"Zoe?" he asks when she bites her lip and looks distressed. "I'm sorry if I've upset you...I didn't mean to..."

"Y.you didn't?" she asks, disappointed yet not really surprised. "Oh. Maybe I should just go." And she makes for the door only to feel his hand reach out and catch her arm.

"Zoe?" Just her name, that's all he says, but the inflection holds a thousand questions.

Again her body takes over her mind, her heart ruling her head and her hormones orchestrating her actions.

His name is a groan on her lips before she claims his and he pulls her tightly into his arms.

Their clothes fly off in all directions and they are thankful that the room comes with a large double bed.

Her breasts, he has seen them before, only hours before down on the beach, but the weight of them fit perfectly in his hands, and he moulds them with a groan of pleasure.

Her moans are electricity along his nerves, her hands fuelling his need of her.

How soft and teasing her lips are on his ear, her tongue thrusting inside to torture and tease him.

When her hand reaches down to feel the length of him, Palmer has to grit his teeth not to lose it right then and there. Her little fingers enclose and excite him, then guide him to the very centre of her heat.

She is hot and wet and her legs are wound around him, struggling to bring him closer to her.

But he manages to stop, look down at her with concern and ask her if she is sure. "I want you badly, Zoe, but only if you're sure?"

"Please," Zoe nods, her breathing shallow gasps, her eyes pools of liquid chocolate.

"Is this your first time?" he asks, wanting to protect and take care if she needs it. But he can't mask his relief when Zoe shakes her head.

He reaches for his pants, pulls on a condom then plunges into her.

Zoe screams, her body arching off the bed and Palmer rides her body like a man possessed.

With each thrust Zoe feels her body respond,

tightening and soaring with need. Palmer is taking her to places she has only read about, imagined, longed for and thought out of her reach. And when she feels his hips beneath her hands tense and shudder, Zoe knows he is close to the edge.

Of their own volition her eyes suddenly open and look deep into his.

At the vital moment they are joined in mind and heart as well as body. Reaching up a hand, Zoe cups his cheek, then slides it back into his hair and bunches it into a fist.

Once, twice, three times more he plunges, deeper every time...and then the heavens open to allow them passage and their bodies begin their blissful descent.

Wrapped tightly together in each other's arms, they fall into sleep with the ease of the innocent. Young love, so shiny and new and all consuming, with so much more to be explored.

CHAPTER EIGHT

A week later and Zoe is getting ready for the firm's barbecue at Dorothy Johnson's house.

Her mother senses that something has changed in Zoe since her return from Italy, but she can't pin it down.

Her daughter is good at keeping her own counsel when she wants to, yet they have always been able to confide in each other when needed.

It is this change, this secretive side of Zoe that has set Carly's alarm bells ringing. Her daughter has been cagey since her return, and that just isn't like Zoe at all.

Dressed in an electric blue mini-dress, Zoe leaves her long auburn hair down and pulls on silver high-heeled sandals.

"There," she says to her reflection in the bedroom mirror. "I think that should do the trick!"

She might be short, but she is slim with a full, firm

bust that is shown off to perfection by the cowl neckline. Her legs look stunning in the four inch stiletto heels and with the tan she gained in Italy.

And if I happen to fall into the boss's arms again...well, so be it! I won't be complaining!

When a car arrives to pick them both up, only Zoe is dressed and ready for the barbecue.

"You still have time to change your mind," Zoe tells her mother. "The invitation was for both of us; it doesn't make sense for you to stay here by yourself."

"Go and enjoy yourself," Carly tells her daughter. "This is your chance to get to know the rest of the people who work for Palmer. I can always come to the next one."

Knowing that she won't be able to change her mother's mind once it is made up, Zoe gives her a hug and makes her way out to the car.

Dorothy comes to the front door to greet her latest guest, and shows Zoe out to the back garden where the barbecue is being worked overtime.

"Hello, Mr Johnson," Zoe greets Palmer's father with a broad smile.

"Just call me Bill, everyone does," he tells her happily. "Can I get you anything," he offers, and uses a spatula to turn the burgers he is grilling.

"Those burgers do look inviting," Zoe smiles. "I

deliberately didn't eat so that I could enjoy the food tonight."

"Good girl, very sensible," he chuckles. "Like some onions on this?" he offers, holding an open cob with a large beef-burger on it.

Frowning, Zoe considers. "I probably shouldn't, but I do love fried onions – let's go for it!"

They both laugh and Palmer smiles broadly as he joins them.

"Nice to see you're enjoying yourself," he tells Zoe, but doesn't move in too close.

"Your father is tempting me with his cooking," she grins impishly. "Not that he's having to try that hard."

"Good to hear, I like a woman with a healthy appetite. Can I get you a glass of wine or something else to go with that?" Palmer offers.

"A glass of wine would be lovely," and Zoe moves with him to sit where he indicates a small table under the shelter of an awning.

As soon as Palmer moves off Connor moves in. Taking a seat by her side, he leans in close. "You look rather stunning tonight," he smiles lasciviously. "Got any plans for later?"

"Plans?" Zoe frowns up at her unexpected company.

"Plans...to get out of here," he adds when she

continues to look confused. "You surely don't intend to stay here all night – not dressed like that!"

His finger slides up her leg to her knee and starts to trail back up to her thigh when she knocks his hand away.

"Don't!" One word, but all her disgust for Palmer's brother is contained in it.

"Only got eyes for the rich man, eh?" And he looks her up and down taking in every line and curve. "You'll soon get bored. Palmer may be rich but he doesn't know how to have a good time. I'll be waiting when you want to live a little," he offers with a wicked wink.

When Palmer returns with her wine, Zoe is so relieved she can barely hide it. "Oh, thank you, Palmer...just what I need!"

With that she takes the glass of wine and half empties it, drawing a frown from Palmer.

"Ah, and there she is," Connor grins over at the woman who has just arrived, "the lovely Laura. Light of my life!"

"Did he do something to upset you?" Palmer asks, sitting in the seat that Connor has just vacated.

Deciding not to cause any more strife between the brothers, Zoe shakes her head. "No, Connor was just asking if we had plans for later. Apparently he thinks the barbecue will be very boring and plans to go out later."

"Typical! Given a chance to mix and socialise with the men he works with and Connor prefers to live it up at some club!" Palmer bites out. "Damned typical!"

"Don't worry about it," Zoe puts a hand to Palmers arm, but withdraws it quickly. "Everyone else seems to be enjoying themselves."

"Is this how it's going to be between us, Zoe?" Palmer frowns as she shifts away in her seat. "Are you ashamed to be seen with me?"

"What? No, of course not," Zoe gapes at her lover, who is also her boss. "But you have to admit, if we're open about our relationship it would be fodder for the gossips. And I don't like being talked about and stared at. Let's just keep it between ourselves – it's no one else's business after all!"

Remaining quiet, Palmer simply nods his head in agreement. But he doesn't like it. Why should they be furtive, sneaking around as they have since their return from Italy? Palmer wants to shout his happiness from the rooftops; he's fallen hook line and sinker for his PA, and doesn't give a stuff what anyone else thinks!

All night he watches Zoe laugh and socialise with the rest of his employees and their families. She is bright, gregarious and funny. And everyone seems to like her.

When his mother comments on that fact, Palmer finds

himself snapping at her. "Isn't she just!" he agrees snippily then has to apologise. "Sorry, mother, I'm just tired and have a lot on my mind."

With a raised brow, Dorothy Johnson looks up at her son and thinks she knows exactly what he has on his mind. "Then go and do something about it," she suggests, her meaning obvious.

"I already have, she just doesn't want anyone else to know about it," he confesses quietly, sadly.

"Hmm, she's in a tricky situation," Dorothy smiles, more content now that she knows what is upsetting her favourite son. "Some people can be judgemental. A secretary falling for her boss is a classic joke that I don't think Zoe would enjoy being the butt of. Just give her time and room to get comfortable with the situation – I'm sure she'll come around in time."

"But in the meantime all the men think she's available, and she damned well isn't!" Palmer declares hotly, watching as Dave Healey makes a move on Zoe.

When he moves to go over and put the man straight, Dorothy puts a restraining hand on his arm. "Just wait and watch – I think Zoe is plenty capable of looking out for herself."

And sure enough, Zoe laughs and pats Dave on the arm, shaking her head at his suggestion of a night out together.

The rest of the men roar with laughter, telling Dave that he's struck out again, but he takes it all in good part.

"There now," Dorothy beams with satisfaction, "what did I tell you!"

But Palmer still isn't happy about it. He wants the world to know that Zoe belongs to him. He wants Connor to know that she is off limits, and watches as his brother sidles up to his woman, even with Laura on his other arm!

When he drives her home, Palmer is quiet, subdued, lost in thought, and Zoe grows concerned.

"Palmer? Is something wrong?"

Pulling up outside her house, he turns in his seat to look at Zoe and doesn't bother to answer. Undoing their seatbelts, he pulls her into his arms and kisses her as though his life depends on it.

He has had to watch her from the sidelines, only able to talk to and touch her as every other man at the barbecue, when all he wanted was to take her in his arms and love her.

His head is spinning with need, his emotions churning up with frustration and pride. Palmer loves her! He really loves her, and Zoe has kept him at arm's length all night!

When he finally raises his head, both of them are gasping for breath, their eyes heated but for very different reasons.

"We...we can't, not here," Zoe gasps, thinking of her mother watching for her return.

"Why?" Palmer demands. "Afraid your mother will see us?" he guesses correctly. "What is it about us that you're trying to hide? We're consenting adults in a normal relationship. One that is beginning to feel very one sided," he tells her angrily.

"I don't know what you mean?" Zoe gasps at his sudden outburst. Her lips are still tingling from his arduous kiss, her heartbeat still fierce and rising in her throat. "I care about you just as much as you care about me, it's just not that easy," she insists, placing her hand over his on her knee.

"Really...why not?" he demands. "I'm sick of seeing other men think it's ok to hit on you. I'm sick of having to sit back and let it happen. And most of all, I'm sick of my brother drooling all over you; looking at you like someone he wants to drag into his bed!"

She's never seen Palmer so angry. And it's her fault, Zoe realises. "I'm sorry, Palmer. I didn't realise I was hurting you like that."

"Damn it, Zoe – I love you!"

They have never said that to each other, and Zoe is shocked to hear him say it now.

"Palmer, you don't have to say that just to make me

go out with you in public," Zoe declares hesitantly.

With a gentle hand on her cheek, Palmer shakes his head in wonder. "I don't know how I haven't realised it before," he tells her softly. "I love you, Zoe Benson, and that is what I want the world to know."

Grinning like a fool, Zoe can only shake her head. She can't believe that she has been so stupid.

But Palmer takes her meaning the wrong way. "You don't feel the same?" he asks, a frown marring his beautiful blue eyes.

"What? Are you crazy?" she gasps, then Zoe flings both arms around his neck and kisses him soundly on the lips. "I love you so much it scares me silly. I was afraid if I told you it would frighten you off!"

"Not on your life! I'm not going anywhere — and neither are you," he declares, and their kiss is fierce, deep, hungry and greedy, then joyful and plain loving.

"We need to have a party," Palmer tells her. And when Zoe frowns he just laughs. "An engagement party — I want you to marry me, Zoe Benson. And I want you wearing my ring before the month is out!"

"But first, we have to tell my mother," and Zoe looks nervously back to the house where her mother is waiting for her return.

"You sound apprehensive — is there something I should know?"

Turning back to Palmer, Zoe frowns and begins her tale.

"My mother was a PA when she met my father," Zoe sighs. "He was an actor and she took care of his mail and organised his life, basically. Apparently he was a real gentleman, full of praise for how my mother kept all the tedious stresses and strains out of his hair and they started to see each other personally."

Stopping, Zoe thinks about the way her father had abandoned her mother in her time of need and isn't sure it is really her tale to tell. "Basically, they married, and when my mother had me he left. Went off with his current leading lady," Zoe wafts a dismissive hand in the air to brush the incident aside.

"What I'm trying to say is..."

"Your mother is going to worry that history is repeating itself," Palmer interrupts. "Well, we're just going to have to prove her wrong!" And he takes her hand and pulls her close again.

"I love you, that is an irrefutable fact," and he punctuates his statement with a kiss. "For tonight, we'll keep this between us, but as soon as we've got a ring I want to announce it to the world.

Tell me you'll let me do that?" he implores and holds her hand up to his lips, kissing the place where his ring will sit.

"Of course I will. I love you too!"

CHAPTER NINE

It has been difficult getting Zoe's mother to agree to the meal out. Palmer's mum and dad were much more open to the idea and looked forward to it.

"Mum, the car will be here soon, can't you just enjoy a night out with your daughter without questioning the why's and wherefore's?"

"I just don't see why the Johnson's would want to have a meal with an employee's mother?" Carly Benson reiterates for the one hundredth time. "I know they're a friendly bunch, but really Zoe, I'm nothing to any of them!"

Thankfully the car sent by Palmer draws up in the drive at the front of the house and any further discussion is halted.

It is a stretched limo and Zoe hears her mother's gasp as they step out of their front door.

Almost running to the car, Zoe grins up at Palmer who has alighted to allow them comfortable access and sneaks a kiss before following Zoe to retake his seat.

Dorothy immediately chats away with Carly, expounding her son's lavish provision of a car and driver for the evening.

"He says it was much more economical than getting two cars for the evening," Dorothy giggles delightedly. "Well, I'm not so sure about that but what a hoot! Isn't this lovely?"

"It certainly is lavish," Carly agrees, looking around her at the leather seating and the bucket of champagne.

Pouring each of them a glass, Palmer hands them around. "To family," he toasts cryptically, and the rest of the occupants of the limo repeat it with a laugh.

By the time they arrive at the restaurant, everyone has had a second glass of champagne and even Carly is feeling more relaxed and chipper.

"This is very good of you," Carly smiles up at Palmer as he offers her his arm to escort her inside.

"Entirely my pleasure, I assure you," Palmer chuckles softly, extending his other arm to Zoe. "I'll be the envy of every man in the room with two beautiful women by my side."

His parents look at each other and Bill gives Dorothy a

sly wink. "And I'll have the best all to myself," he tells his wife, and receives a broad smile in return.

The meal is exquisite and the wine has flowed freely all evening. Even Palmer is feeling a little bit tipsy by the time he signals his announcement.

Standing, Palmer looks down at his parents, Zoe and her mother, and feels the knot in his stomach clench tighter.

He has never contemplated anything more important in his life, and he wants to do this right.

"Mum, dad, Carly, I'd like you to bear witness to the most important question I will ever ask anyone," and Palmer moves to stand by Zoe's side.

Dropping to one knee he takes Zoe's hand and says, "Zoe Amelia Benson, I love you more than life, more than I can ever find the words to tell you — please, will you consent to be my wife?"

The restaurant has fallen silent; her mother looks shocked and pale, while Palmer's parents look absolutely delighted. Zoe can hardly breath, she never dreamed he would propose in such a public manner, but delights everyone when she says, "Yes!"

A loud cheer goes up as Palmer slips the ring onto Zoe's finger then catches her up in his arms and twirls her around. And Zoe's head falls back on an exuberant giggling laugh.

The management send over another bottle of champagne on the house, to celebrate the happy couple.

"You should have invited Connor," Dorothy Johnson reproves Palmer when at last they sit down.

"I did, mother, but you know Connor," Palmer continues to smile radiantly, "he always has other plans."

But Zoe can't bring herself to regret Connor's absence. She finds him a little scary and sometimes intimidating and definitely sleazy.

No, tonight she wants to be happy without reservation. This is hers and Palmer's night and one she will always remember with love.

Like a married couple, Palmer and Zoe have planned a weekend away. Neither of them wants to explain themselves to family and friends just yet.

The limo takes their parents' home and a sleek black Mercedes takes them on a long drive down to Cornwall. Her case already stowed in its boot, Zoe snuggles up to her fiancé and sighs.

"I can't remember ever being so happy," she tells Palmer. "Even my mother wished us well before the limo took our parents' home."

"Wow, that's something indeed!" he smiles, caressing her cheek with a gentle thumb. "Do you think she will ever forgive me for daring to claim her daughter for my wife?"

"As long as you make her daughter happy she will," Zoe laughs. "And you certainly did tonight – thank you for all of this," she waves a hand around the splendour of their Mercedes and brings it to rest on his chest next to her cheek.

With an arm holding her against him, Zoe listens to the beat of Palmer's heart and eventually drifts off to sleep.

It is dark as pitch when they pull up outside of a tiny cottage. The driver rounds the car and lifts their luggage from the boot and carries it to the front door. Then he returns and holds the car door open for them to alight.

"Zoe, come on sleepy-head, we're here," Palmer nudges her awake and receives a sleepy yawn for his trouble.

Zoe laughs; "Sorry about that – I blame it on all the booze." And indeed, she is a little unsteady on her feet once they get out of the car and begin walking down the little path to the cottage.

"I do believe you're a bit tipsy, Miss Benson," Palmer rebukes her playfully.

"And you got me this way, so you'd better not be complaining," Zoe tells him while jabbing her finger into his chest.

The driver helps them inside with their luggage then

leaves them to enjoy their weekend away.

With the door closed they are finally alone.

"I love you, Palmer Johnson," Zoe proclaims, flinging her arms around his neck and kissing his lips loudly.

Laughing, he scoops her up and carries her into the sitting room then deposits her, none too gently, on the settee.

Landing with a bounce, Zoe laughs and hiccups then welcomes Palmer into her arms as he sits beside her.

No words now, just happiness and feelings and eventually wants and needs and the willingness to fulfil them.

Each is in the other's embrace, both wanting to show the depth of their love. Their hands explore, gentle and savage in their quest to give pleasure, to feel the other's passions rise in response to their touch.

Only those hands in those intimate places will do. It is Palmer she wants to taste her breasts, to tease their hardened peaks with his lips and deft tongue.

It is Zoe's fingers Palmer wants to feel encircle his engorged length, to fill his mind with erotic thoughts of her surrounding him as he pushes into her heat.

The night is young, and so are they, with their passions unleashed Zoe and Palmer begin exploring the house. They make love in the lounge, then on the stairs, then on the landing and finally in the bed.

"If we keep this pace up," Palmer gasps, "our driver will find us dead from exhaustion come Monday morning!"

"Oh lordy, lordy," Zoe chuckles deeply, "what a way to go!"

"Come," Palmer holds his arm out for Zoe to settle into. She climbs from atop him and instead lies along the length of his side with her head against his heart and his strong arm around her.

"I love listening to your heartbeat, it's so strong and it's galloping at the minute," she chuckles again.

"You make me so happy, Zoe," Palmer tells her, tightening his arm to hug her to him. "I've never felt so alive since the moment you fell out of that lift and into my arms. I knew right then that you were a perfect fit; funny, full of life, and nervous as a kitten if I remember rightly?"

"I was terrified," Zoe tells him. "I had already been for a number of interviews and failed at them all. But yours was the one I really wanted, so that put me under even more pressure."

"Why was that?"

"Because I wanted it so bad," Zoe frowns up at him confused.

"No," and he tickles her side, making her squirm

against him, "why did you want the job with us so bad? We're just another construction company."

Pulling herself up to lean on her elbow, Zoe frowns down at her man.

"Not on your life! Your company has grown from nothing into something in just five years. Officially," she adds, and makes him frown.

"Officially?"

"Well, yes. You did an apprenticeship and then started doing a few jobs in your own right," she states knowledgeably. "But it wasn't until five years ago that you officially became Johnson Construction Company, and my boss," she giggles, bending to kiss his chest.

"You really did your homework – I'm impressed!" he tells her.

"Well, now you can impress me," she smiles sexily and slides over his firmly contoured chest to lie atop him again. "I'm not done yet."

With that, she slides down his body and tastes herself on the hardening length of him and feels him swell rapidly in her mouth.

CHAPTER TEN

When she awakes in the morning, Zoe finds herself sprawled across an otherwise empty bed and wonders where Palmer has gone.

There you are, Adonis personified! Naked and glorious with all that sun shining around you; what's so interesting out there?

Moving silently, Zoe walks up to the back of Palmer and encircles his waist with her arms. In her bare feet she doesn't even reach his shoulders, and he looks down at her with a huge smile.

"The mighty atom has awoken," he states playfully, and gets a dig in the ribs for his trouble.

"My mother always tells me that good things come in small packages!"

"Good? I think she meant awesome, wonderful or

maybe spectacular," he tells her, and kisses Zoe between each superlative. "To me, you're just perfect."

"That is perfect," and Zoe lifts her chin to indicate the dramatic view sprawled out before them. "This cottage and that view are so perfect."

"I can't disagree with you." And Palmer fills his lungs with the fresh sea air.

"How did you know about this place?"

"I searched the internet," he tells her proudly. "I think I put something like 'romantic, cottage, sea-view' into the search engine, then sifted through the results to find this one. It is perfect, isn't it?" he smiles down at her, his eyes adoring every inch and curve.

"No one has ever done anything like this for me before," she looks up, returning his adoration tenfold. "I never dreamed anyone ever would."

"Let's get dressed and start exploring our little paradise, then we can get breakfast and go further afield," Palmer suggests.

Hand in hand, and naked as the day they were born, the two walk into the bathroom and take a very, very long shower together.

Monday comes around all too soon. Their weekend 'honeymoon' had been glorious. But now there is serious work to be done.

Zoe sorts the post, answers the phone, takes dictation and types up more tenders. It is a nonstop hive of activity that leaves her feeling tired but content.

Going through to accounts, Zoe walks up to Laura's desk and deliberately uses her left hand to give her a small pile of letters.

Looking up, Laura makes to take the letters then notices the ring Zoe is wearing.

"What the hell?!" she gasps, then stands quickly to pull Zoe in for a hug. "You got engaged? But you've only known each other a few weeks?"

Laughing, Zoe holds out her hand for Laura to examine. "When you know you know – we just clicked and couldn't keep our hands off each other!"

"Oh. My. God." Laura gapes, turning Zoe's hand this way and that to see the row of three beautiful diamonds glimmer in the sunlight. "Does Connor know? He didn't say anything when I saw him Saturday."

"Palmer invited him to the meal out on Friday when we made the announcement, but he said he was busy," Zoe tells her. "But I would have thought he'd have seen his parents by Saturday."

Frowning, Laura sits back down in her seat and Zoe pulls up a chair.

"He's been acting really strange lately. He meets up

with people who don't seem to be friends," Laura observes. "More like some kind of business thing, if you know what I mean?"

"Business? You think Connor is branching out on his own?" Zoe asks, not able to hide her delight at the prospect.

"Well if he is, I can't imagine what he's branching out into," Laura scoffs. "I mean, he hates the construction industry. He never stops telling me how much he hates working for Palmer!"

Realising who she is talking to, Laura smiles apologetically, "Sorry, that sounded mean, but I just meant to say, I can't imagine Connor branching out on his own in that particular direction."

"Then, what else could it be?" Zoe asks, a niggling worry building at the back of her mind.

"Believe me, I have no idea," Laura exclaims, throwing her hands palms up in the air. "We might be seeing a bit of each other lately, but Connor is a closed book. He tells me nothing!"

Walking back to her office, Zoe mulls over what Laura has told her and the uneasy feeling in her gut gnaws at her.

I just hope he hasn't gotten into anything illegal, Palmer would be gutted. And so would his mother. Damn you, Connor!

Today they have received a reply from the Rodriguez Hotel owners. If Palmer wants the job, it is his.

Casting off her gloomy mood, Zoe thinks about the Italian hotel and is too excited to wait for Palmer to come back in to the office. Instead she calls his mobile to give him the news.

"I would love to take it on," he tells her, "I'm just not sure who I can spare to send over there. I mean, with Connor playing up I can't send Craig, and he would have been my first choice!"

"Hmm, he can certainly run a job – the Dersinger project has come on leaps and bounds since he took over it," Zoe confirms, having spoken to Terry Fielding, the project's architect just that morning.

"The annoying thing is he could be good if he actually put his mind to it," Palmer sighs heavily. "He just wants to swan around in a suit all day doing as little as possible."

She's tempted to tell Palmer that he isn't responsible for babying Connor through his worthless life, but just can't bear to upset him.

"Maybe he'll grow out of it," Zoe suggests, cringing on her end of the phone, glad that Palmer can't see her red face.

"Grow out of it...?" Palmer laughs, then laughs a lot more. "Only you, Zoe."

"Well, I just meant...maybe...when he meets a nice girl and settles down he'll become more responsible...or something."

"Ok, that's it!" she tells him when Palmer continues to laugh.

"Well, we are talking about Connor," Palmer finally stops laughing.

"And he's your brother, not your son," Zoe tells him, and could have bitten her tongue off.

"You think I should cut him loose," Palmer states rather than asks. "And I would, but it would kill my mother."

"I know, and I'm sorry for saying anything, I just know how much you would love to do the Italian job."

"Let me think about it," Palmer suggests. "There has to be something I can put him on that he won't screw up!"

She doesn't see Palmer before end of day, and takes the lift down to the ground floor by herself.

Holding her car keys out in front of her, Zoe presses the button to unlock it and hears the familiar thud. But another sound has her spinning on her heels.

"Connor! You scared the life out of me!"

His smile is sneering, and he doesn't look quite himself. "So, big brother has put his ring on you," he snarls, grabbing her hand and raising it to look at her ring finger. "Christ! He doesn't do things by halves, does he? Must have cost him a bloody fortune!"

"Why should you care?" Zoe snatches her hand back and begins to open her car door, but Connor isn't finished.

Pushing her back against it, Connor traps her against the car door. "I'll be able to give you more than that in a few months' time," he tells her cryptically. "A poxy ring with a few stones in it will be small change after I get done!"

"Get done doing what?" she asks, remembering what Laura had told her.

"Never you mind — but I won't be swinging a fucking pickaxe for much longer. That's for god damned sure!" And Connor laughs, his eyes not bothering to conceal the anger.

Then he does something that Zoe couldn't have anticipated, wouldn't have suspected Connor intended.

He kissed her! But it wasn't just a peck on the cheek, or even the kind of kiss you might give a girl you're interested in after a first date.

No, his lips were fierce on hers, possessive and demanding. His hand cupped her breast, not gently, not caressingly, but bruisingly hard and insistent.

Twisting her mouth away from his she begs, "Connor, stop! Please stop!"

"I could make you beg for me to take you," he sneers angrily. "You think big brother can show you a good time – think again. He's nothing! Nobody! And you'll come to see that in time...then I'll be waiting!"

Wiping the back of her hand across her mouth, Zoe tries desperately not to cry. "You'll never be half the man Palmer is! So go hold your breath while you wait for me to come to you – you'll die waiting for me!"

With that, Zoe pulls her car door open and cracks Connor on the knee. With a hysterical chuckle, she starts the car and pulls away before he can do anything to stop her. But she doesn't get far. Turning the next corner she brings the car to a halt and turns off the engine.

Oh God! Oh God! Please God help me! I don't know what just happened. Did I do something to make him think I wanted that? At the barbecue...did I say or do something to make him think I wanted him?

I don't know...I don't know...I don't think so...but I don't know.

Tears overwhelm her, slide down Zoe's pale cheeks in unchecked torrents. And the sobs tear from her in gulping, rasping groans of anguish.

What do I do? What do I do? Call Palmer...? Taking her mobile from her shoulder bag, Zoe sits staring at it. *What can I say? Will he think I encouraged him? Will he think I actually wanted Connor to do that?*

She feels nauseated by the thought and has to open the car door to pull in some fresh air.

Oh, Palmer...Palmer. I don't know what to do. I don't understand what just happened!

When she eventually gets home, Zoe makes the excuse that she is coming down with something and goes straight to her room.

A shower...I just need to clear my head and wash the feel of him off me!

But it isn't that easy. She brushes her teeth three times; stands under the shower for half an hour, but still Zoe can feel and taste Connor Johnson.

Laying on her back, Zoe stares up at her bedroom ceiling and clutches the quilt to her.

What about tomorrow? How can I go back? How can I continue working for Palmer when his brother is such a pig! He could meet me out of work any time. He could do exactly what he did tonight and maybe even worse.

Oh God! Is that where this is leading? Does Connor intend to rape me?

<u>CHAPTER ELEVEN</u>

A week passes with no further incidents with Connor. Zoe had woken up the next day determined not to let him drive her away.

This is her dream job and she has worked hard to secure it. And she loves Palmer. She can't hold him responsible for his brother's lack of morals.

But it has been difficult to relax with Palmer since the assault. Their physical relationship has suffered with Zoe telling him that she hasn't been feeling well lately.

She can't put him off forever, she knows, and Zoe doesn't really want to; she just has to get the image of Connor pawing at her out of her head.

"I've decided to take the Italian job on," Palmer smiles over his desk at her as Zoe walks into his office.

She beams at him, then frowns uncertainly, "So, you've solved your problem with Connor?"

"Not exactly," he tells her, and rubs his chin with a bemused look on his handsome face. "I can't put my finger on it, but he seems to be on his best behaviour. He's done more work in this past week than in all the time he's worked for me," Palmer laughs.

"Maybe you were right after all. Maybe seeing Laura is settling him down," he tells her, an eyebrow raised in question.

"Maybe," Zoe readily agrees. *Or maybe he's just feeling guilty! And so you should, you filthy pig!*

"Have you been to the doctors yet?" Palmer asks, his brows drawn in concern at her continued pallor.

"Don't worry about me, I'm feeling better every day." And she is, she realises, smiling and walking to his side.

Swivelling his chair to better face her, Palmer pulls her into his lap.

"Palmer, no!" Zoe screeches, trying to jump up quickly. But his arms are strong and hold her fast.

"I thought this was one of the boss's perks," he tells her, pulling her in for a kiss.

Getting her breath back, Zoe finally gets up and straightens her skirt. "It had better not be," she chuckles playfully. "Not with anyone but me, at any rate." Then she raises an eyebrow at him and looks suitably stern, "Did you ever do that with any of your other secretaries?"

Palmer's jaw drops and his eyes go wide. "What? No! Never!"

"Hmm," Zoe eyes him speculatively, keeping her face as straight as possible, "I wonder? You were pretty slick with that move – some might say practiced!"

Cheeks paling now, Palmer holds up both hand in surrender. "I'm telling you, Zoe..."

But she can't keep her face straight any longer and bursts into a fit of the giggles.

"So...," he stands and walks towards her menacingly, "...you're playing with me, huh?" And reaching for her, he traps her with one arm and tickles her with his other hand.

"What's this, and I was feeling sorry for you both being cooped up in an office on such a lovely day," Dorothy Johnson gives them an indulgent mother's smile. "Now put Zoe down and behave yourself," she tells Palmer.

"I'll bet dad got you in a clinch or two when you worked for him," Palmer grins at his mother with a knowing glint in his adoring blue eyes.

"I'll have you know your father was a gentleman at all times, in the office," she tells him, her chin going up but turning her head enough to give Zoe a secret wink.

"Well, what can I do for you, mother? I don't usually

get the pleasure of your company at work," he tells her, and pulls a chair up for her to take a seat.

"No, don't go my dear, you're part of the family now," Dorothy smiles fondly at Zoe. "But I would appreciate it if you would close the door."

Palmer retakes the seat behind his desk and pats his knee for Zoe to sit. Blushing, she does so, but just on the edge and very reluctantly.

"It's Connor," Dorothy begins with a sigh. "I don't know what's wrong but something definitely is."

"What do you mean? Is he causing trouble at home or just not coming home?" Palmer asks confused.

"Oh, he stays out just as often as he ever has, but when he does come home he's different!"

"Different how, mother? You're being very vague."

"Different in that he is...different!" Dorothy flounders to explain. "One minute he's sullen and the next he's angry. He's different!" she states again.

"What exactly are you trying to say? Do you think he's on drugs?"

Zoe feels her heart plummet and her hands clench. *Is that what I saw? Different is exactly what I thought when he trapped me in the car park. Was Connor on drugs then?!*

"Palmer!" his mother rebukes sharply. But then

Dorothy looks at her son and deep concern etches her eyes. "I didn't think of that...it never occurred to me. Oh, Palmer, do you think that's it? Do you think Connor could be mixed up in drugs?"

Zoe stands, moves around the desk and lays a hand on Dorothy's shoulder. "Please, let me get you a cup of tea. Palmer will sort things out, don't worry," she smiles kindly at the older woman and prays she is right.

Palmer doesn't stop her leaving the office, obviously wanting to talk to his mother alone.

When Zoe enters the kitchen she sees Laura in there making herself a cup of coffee. "Hi, how are you doing?" she asks, then gasps when the other woman turns to look at her.

"Laura, what on earth – are you alright?"

Laura has a black eye and no amount of make-up has been able to cover it up.

"I just turned into my wardrobe door," she says, holding a hand over the bruised eye. "I almost didn't come in today; I knew it would look bad."

Was this just a coincidence, or had Connor done this to Laura? "Laura, you'd tell me if someone hurt you, right?"

But Laura just rolls her eyes and laughs, "I told you, me and the wardrobe door just had a falling out. Believe me, I wacked it good and proper after my head stopped spinning!"

"Ok," Zoe smiles, though she still isn't sure that she believes her. "Are you really ok to be here? It looks hellish painful."

Picking up her mug of coffee, Laura gives Zoe her best smile. "I'm fine, you're worse than my mother. She almost marched me off to the docs till I told her I had to get to work."

"Ok. If you're sure," Zoe turns and watches Laura go back to the accounts office.

Taking a tray with three cups of tea on it back to Palmer's office, Zoe gives a perfunctory knock and enters.

"Here you go," and she hands a cup to Dorothy and one to Palmer.

"As I was telling Zoe earlier, Connor has been working really hard this past week – I'm surprised by all this," Palmer declares with a shake of his head.

"Maybe I'm worrying about nothing," Dorothy smiles, and thanks Zoe for the tea. "I've never had a day's worth or worry about Palmer – but Connor," She raises her eyes to the heavens and gives a despairing shake of her head, "I never seem to stop worrying about that boy!"

After Dorothy Johnson left, Zoe goes back to work but can't concentrate.

Is this my opportunity to tell Palmer about Connor assaulting me?

And what about Laura – did she really get that black eye from the wardrobe door, or did Connor do that to her?

If I go to Palmer now what will he do? He might even get angry at me for not telling him before!

Maybe I should just watch and wait. If Laura gets any more bruises I'll definitely talk to Palmer!

She is going to his flat tonight. It is huge, the whole of the top floor of an old factory conversion. It is called a 'loft' apartment, and Zoe loves it.

Standing at one of the floor to ceiling windows, she can see right across the city. All the street lights and windows are gleaming like jewels.

"It's so beautiful up here," she murmurs. "Did you convert this building into flats?"

"No," Palmer answers, putting an arm around her waist he moves to stand next to her. "But I'd like to do something similar when I get the chance."

Turning into him, Zoe buries her face in his chest and inhales him deeply. She loves the male scent of him, and finally feels free of Connor.

"Take me to bed, Palmer," Zoe lifts her face to his and watches his lower to kiss her. "I've missed you," she sighs, when he lifts his head again, and puts her hand in his.

The loft is completely open. No doors, no separate rooms, except for the bathroom at the far end.

Instead the loft Is subtly zoned. The kitchen Is built into a corner with a dining table and chairs set in the middle of the space. A couple of wardrobes are set against a wall next to the king-sized bed, and two four-seater settees and a couple of armchairs make up the living area with a glass-topped coffee table forming a central island.

But best of all, to Zoe's way of thinking, are the extensive floor-to-ceiling windows that give an unobstructed view out over the city. They have no curtains or blinds, there is no need.

And when she stands naked next to them, she actually feels liberated.

There is no one to see them. No need to cover up for fear of prying eyes. So when he cups her breasts then falls to his knees in front of her, Zoe doesn't feel embarrassed or shy, she feels wonderfully free spirited and thankful.

Thankful that the memory of Connor is finally fading, and her love of Palmer is strong enough to wipe it clean away.

They love well, and long, enjoying the touch and feel of the other's body. Moans are exchanged, guttural gasps rent the air and nothing could be more natural.

When his tongue probes her ear she shudders, when his fingers delve deep inside her she arches, but when he takes her, when he pushes himself deep inside of her, she braces and answers him beat for thrusting beat.

This is what she has missed. They are a physical couple and she has denied Palmer and herself this wonderful pleasure.

But no more! To hell with Connor, this is who they are and she will not allow him to come between them ever again!

Curling into Palmer, Zoe kisses his chest and moans, "I love you so much. You wouldn't believe how lucky I feel right now."

"You're not the only one," Palmer tells her, placing a kiss on the top of her head and stroking her long auburn hair. "I began to wonder if I'd ever meet anyone I'd want to marry – but I knew right off you were special."

She yawns and stretches like a cat, then snuggles in and falls asleep.

For the last week she has been wakeful, her dreams dark and fearful, but not tonight. She sleeps like a baby and wakes to another sunny day in busy Birmingham.

CHAPTER TWELVE

Lawson Street, Birmingham. When Connor wakes up it is dark and cold and the ground beneath him is hard as rock.

In fact, it is concrete. He rolls onto his side and feels stones dig into his thigh as he does so.

"Where the fuck?"

He sits up, looks around and sees that he is in the middle of an empty car park. But it won't be empty for long. This is Birmingham, a busy city where parking is prime no matter what day of the week.

And what day is it? For fuck's sake, I can't remember a damn thing!

Staggering to his feet, Connor brushes himself off and notices a few bruised areas.

"God damn it!" His jeans are torn on one knee; his

jacket has deep scuff marks on the elbows and across his shoulders and his shoes look like he's been dragged while wearing them.

Putting a hand to his throbbing forehead, Connor tries to think back.

He can remember the Penny-farthing bar. Chas Davey had been in there and so had Mark Haynes. They'd had a few drinks together...

"Christ! David Hickey!"

That prick! He could have given me more time. I told him I'd have some money for his boss by the end of the month.

The whole alcohol blurred memory starts to come back to him. But it is sketchy.

Basically, Hickey had taken him out back of the bar, had demanded his boss's money and had knocked seven bells out of Connor when he'd told him he didn't have it yet. But he would, he just needed some time was all.

The rest was hazy. How he'd ended up in the car park in Lawson Street was anyone's guess.

And how he'd get home was also anyone's guess.

Connor felt in his pockets, his mobile was gone, his wallet was gone, but he found a small amount of change in the lining of his jacket.

"Laura, come pick me up," Connor mumbles into the

mobile he'd paid a kid three pounds and change to use. "I'm at Lancaster Circus Queensway, standing on the corner of Lancaster Street near the subway."

Half an hour later Connor spots Laura's car coming around the large junction.

He moves to the edge of the road and climbs into her car as soon as she pulls up.

"What the hell, Connor? Where's your car?" Laura asks, not having taken a proper look at his clothing.

"I haven't a clue," Connor grinds out, annoyed by the irritation in her voice. "But you can bet I wouldn't have called you to pick me up if I had it, now would I?"

Deciding that riling Connor would only bring its own brand of trouble, Laura falls silent and concentrates on driving.

"Am I taking you home, or what?" she asks eventually.

Remembering how he looks, Connor has to think about it.

"No, take me to Mark Haynes', he's about the same size as me I can borrow some of his clothes!"

Only then does Laura turn enough to take in Connor's dishevelled appearance.

"Christ, Connor! You look awful!"

"Hence I don't want to go home yet," he snaps. Then he takes a couple of steadying breaths and puts a hand on her knee. "Just help me out here, Laura. I can't remember half of what happened last night – so if I don't know I can't tell you, now can I?"

"I suppose not," she mumbles. She really likes Connor – when he's not being an arsehole he's mostly really nice. "Were you out with Mark last night?"

Rubbing a hand over his eyes, Connor yawns and leans his head back in the seat. "Started out that way. Maybe he knows what happened to me?"

Laura pulls up outside the block of flats where Mark lives. She walks into the lift lobby with Connor and they go up to the fourth floor.

Knocking on the door, Connor yelps and gives his hand a shake, "Shit!" The knuckles are grazed and sore. Changing to a closed fist, he hammers on the door.

"Ok. What the fuck?" calls an annoyed voice from behind the closed door.

When it opens, Mark looks surprised to see Connor standing at his door.

"Jesus-H-Christ, I thought you were dead for sure!" Mark stands back to allow the pair entry, then says, "You must have someone watching over you – when Hickey came back into the pub he was boasting that he'd left you for dead!"

So it was Hickey that dumped me in that car park! I'll get that bastard back if it's the last thing I do!

"Was my car still there when you left?" Connor asks, still not able to fill in the blanks.

"Hickey had your car keys, your mobile and your wallet," Mark tells him. "From what I heard while he was boasting at the bar, he was taking the car back to his boss to clear off some debt you owed."

"Fuck!" Connor explodes. "I told that dip-shit I'd have his money by the end of the month...with interest, damn it!"

"You should never have gotten into bed with Jennings," Mark tells him. "I told you right off the bat, that betting with him was going to be more trouble than it was worth!"

"Really! Well I suppose now you get to say I told you so," Connor sneers. "Don't you have any coffee – my head's fucking killing me!"

"Did you take a look at your face?" Mark asks, standing to move over to his kitchenette. "It looks like somebody stomped on your head!"

Connor looks at Laura, and she nods in agreement. Getting up, Connor strides over to the bathroom and both Laura and Mark cringe at the language that comes out of it.

"I'm gonna kill that bastard! I swear on my mother's life, I'm gonna kill David Hickey!"

"Here," Mark holds out a mug of strong black coffee to Connor and a mug of tea for Laura. "Don't start bad mouthing Hickey, and especially not Jennings. You'll end up deader than a rock if you do."

"No," Connor was holding a face cloth soaked in cold water to his swollen lip, "I'm not as stupid as Hickey – if I'm going to bring him down I won't go broadcasting it all over the city. But there are ways and means of wiping the floor with his sort, and I'll be looking into them for sure!"

Zoe is spending the weekend at Palmer's place. They mostly snuggle up on the settee and watch films on his wall mounted flat screen TV. But occasionally they cook, or go out to eat.

She loves the café culture that is rife in Birmingham. They'd sit outside and chat over coffee for a while, watching the world go by. Then go back to the flat for a bout of nookie and another film.

"I feel like a complete slug, just vegging out for the whole weekend," Zoe groans, rolling over to lie atop of Palmer on the settee.

"It isn't often I get to do it, so make the most of it," he tells her. "I'm usually checking on various sites that we have working, or looking over new ones to price them up."

"Really? So, I'll get to see more of you at work than at home," Zoe states, astonished by the fact.

"Home...I like the sound of that," Palmer smiles and runs a hand down her back to her pert little bottom. "You should move in with me; then we can see each other in the mornings and go into work together. Don't you think?"

With her mouth falling open, Zoe tries to think. "I...I don't know. My mother might have a thing or two to say about that!"

"Hmm, not that I want to get on your mum's bad side, but you are twenty – old enough to make up your own mind," Palmer suggests.

"Yes, and I would, if I weren't leaving her on her own," Zoe frowns, knowing that the day will come sooner or later. "I don't think she really liked me staying over with you the whole weekend, but she didn't give me any grief over it."

"So what about when we get married?" he asks, pulling himself more upright and bringing her with him.

"I know, I've often wished she would meet someone," Zoe tells him. "But if she never goes out how the heck can that happen?"

"We'll have to make it happen," Palmer grins. "We'll invite some eligible bachelors over for a meal and make sure your mother is here too. Then, voila, we'll all be happy!"

Zoe giggles and shakes her head. "My mother on a blind date – I just can't see it!"

"No. No. It has to be our secret," he tells her conspiratorially. "We'll just invite her over for dinner and just happen to have a couple of similarly aged gentlemen over at the same time. Though we'll have to be canny about it, or she won't accept again after the first time!"

Back in the office on Monday, Zoe is sorting the post when Connor walks in. His face is still bruised and he barely looks at her as he marches through to Palmer's office.

Only seconds later he's back, standing tall and annoyed in front of her desk.

"Where is he?!" Connor demands.

This is the first time she's seen Connor since he assaulted her, and he doesn't even make any attempt to apologise.

"If you had waited I could have told you that your brother isn't in," Zoe looks up stonily, her voice as cold as ice.

"I get that, now where is he?!" His voice has grown louder but Zoe stands, determined to show Connor that he can't intimidate her.

"He went straight to the Dersinger site, where you should be working," she states, her brown eyes hard as nails.

"I came into work with Laura – I'll have to take a works van to get over there."

Without a please or thank you he just holds out his hand for a set of keys. "You'll have to pick the keys up from reception on the ground floor and sign them out," she tells him, and has the pleasure of watching him flush.

He drops his hand and just looks at her. "You think you're so much better than the rest of us. But one of these days you'll fall off that pedestal and come a cropper, and I'll be there to watch."

Without another word, Connor turns on his heels and stomps out of her office.

What the hell does Laura see in that ape? And who did that to his face – there's obviously someone else who detests Connor besides me?

Taking the post through to accounts, Zoe takes the chance to ask Laura about him.

"Connor just came in for some van key," she tells Laura. "Have you seen him this weekend?"

The other girl blushes, and Zoe knows that she has. "He got into some sort of fight," Laura explains, taking the post from Zoe and not expounding. "I only saw him when he called for me to pick him up."

Looking at Laura, searching for any sign of new injuries, Zoe tries to be tactful. "Laura, you are such a lovely woman, why would you saddle yourself with Connor? He isn't nearly good enough for you."

"Well we can't all hook millionaires," Laura snaps uncharacteristically. Then she looks up and her bottom lip trembles treacherously, "I'm sorry, I think I love the jerk! But he has this 'thing' about Palmer, goes on about being richer than him some day – though I don't know how he plans to do it!" She laughs, and then breaks down in tears.

"I don't know what to do," Laura admits. "He got beat up this weekend because he owes someone a lot of money, and apparently they thought they'd left him for dead – so it has to be really serious!"

"Holy shit!" Zoe exclaims. "We need to tell Palmer. His mother was in here the other day telling him that she's worried about Connor. Is he into drugs?" she asks, and watches Laura blanch telling her all she needs to know.

"I'm not sure about drugs," Laura confesses, "but he's gambling a lot. That's why he got beat up; he owes some bigwig a lot of money."

CHAPTER THIRTEEN

Going in to Palmer's office, Zoe closes the door for privacy in the hopes that no one will dare to walk in.

Then she calls Palmer on his mobile.

"Hi," he greets her cheerfully, "are you ok?"

"I'm fine," she tells him, and sounds anything but. "Palmer, I need to talk to you, but not on the phone. Can you come back to the office?"

The phone stays quiet so long that Zoe begins to think she's been cut off.

"Palmer...?"

"Is this about us? Did something happen?"

"I...I don't know what you mean," Zoe tells him hesitantly, worried she might say the wrong thing.

"I've tried not to dwell on it, Zoe, but you've been keeping me at a distance lately – I just don't want anything to come between us. Ok?"

"No. Oh no, that's not it at all," Zoe assures him. "But it is serious Palmer. I really do need to talk to you."

She hears his loud expelling of air, and knows she just put him through hell.

"I'm on my way. I'll be back in the office in about an hour," he tells her. "Will that do?"

"Yes. Palmer...I love you – please don't race back and end up in a crash!"

"Damn it, Zoe! I thought... Damn it!" Then the line goes dead and Zoe just stares at her mobile.

He makes it back in forty minutes and looks fraught with worry.

She trails after Palmer into his office and watches as he takes off his tool belt and pours himself a whisky.

He downs it in one gulp, then turns to stare at Zoe.

"What's going on? If you want out of this relationship then just tell me straight!"

Shaking her head, Zoe crosses the room and takes his face between her hands. "I love you – I told you, this has nothing to do with us. Well, mostly...anyway."

"Zoe, you're driving me crazy..."

"It's Connor!" Zoe blurts out, and watches Palmer take a step back. "He's in trouble, Palmer."

Before he can discuss Connor he needs to feel Zoe in his arms and pulls her into him then just holds her.

"Jesus, Zoe." Just that. Just her name whispered into her hair, and he might as well have quoted poetry to her, it feels so good.

"Don't ever think like that, Palmer. I just couldn't tell you over the phone – it's really bad," she warns him.

"Ok," he pulls back but doesn't let her go. When he sits in his seat he pulls her down with him. "So what has little brother been up to now?"

Oh lord! Where do I start? Do I tell him about the car park...about what I suspect about Laura's black eye, or do I just stick to what happened this weekend.

He can see the wheels turning in her head and braces himself for the worst.

"Just tell me, Zoe. Has he done something illegal?"

"I need to get up," she tells him, and pushes off his knee. Then Zoe walks around his desk and clasps her hands.

"You remember when I wasn't feeling well...when we didn't...we didn't make love for a while?" she asks him hesitantly.

His eyes narrow, but he doesn't say anything, just nods and waits for her to continue.

"Well...I wasn't sick...not exactly." Her hands are twisting nervously in front of her, and she has begun to pace his office.

"That Friday, I was the last to leave so I locked up and put the alarm on as usual then went to my car. But just as I unlocked the door someone grabbed me from behind...and I...I...I was scared..."

"Connor! I'll kill him!" Palmer rages, his face twisting with it.

"Yes, it was Connor," she confirms, and finds it difficult to continue. "He said a lot of things, heated things, hateful things...and then he kissed me," and without realising she wipes the back of her hand across her mouth, while her other hand covers the breast he'd mauled.

The moves aren't missed by Palmer and he realises the extent of Connor's assault. "Did he rape you?" His voice has gone deathly quiet and his eyes are livid.

"No. No, Palmer, he didn't!" she tells him quickly. "He just...he made me feel...dirty. Horribly, filthy, dirty."

Palmer stands up, but doesn't immediately go to Zoe. "Is there more, or is that it?"

"There's more," she tells him quietly. "When your mother was here the other day, when she spoke to you about Connor," and he nods to let her know he remembers when she's talking about. "When I went to make the tea, I saw Laura in the kitchen – she had a black eye, Palmer. And I suspect it was Connor who gave it to her."

"Jesus fucking Christ!" he explodes, and runs a hand back through his hair and clenches it at the roots. "Is she alright? Why didn't Laura come to me – is she frightened to speak to me?"

"She didn't admit that it was Connor," Zoe tells him. "She said she walked into her wardrobe door."

"Huh! I'll buy that when all hell freezes over," he exclaims angrily. "Was that the first time, or were there other injuries you think she may have lied about?"

"I've been paying particular attention, and I haven't seen anything else. But-," Zoe hesitates; worried about the damage she is doing to the brother's relationship. "Palmer, he was beaten up really badly this weekend – the people who did it thought they'd left him for dead. It seems he owes money to the wrong kind of people – apparently, he's been gambling pretty heavily."

"This just keeps getting better and better! Is Laura in today?" he asks, trying to keep control of his mangled emotions.

Nodding, Zoe says, "She loves him, Palmer, and I think she's genuinely frightened for him. And so am I."

"You! Why on earth would you be frightened for him?!"

"I may not like what he did, but he doesn't deserve to die!"

Hauling in a breath and letting it whoosh out, Palmer tries to take it all in. "Damn it! Now what?!"

"He came in with Laura this morning and took one of the firm's vans to get to the site – I don't know what's happened to his car," she tells him.

"Oh for crying out loud, that was a mega expensive luxury that he spent most of his inheritance on!" Slumping down in his seat, Palmer pulls all his emotions in and starts putting his thoughts together.

"Give me some time to think things through and make a plan," Palmer tells her. "And don't let Laura go home without seeing me first!"

Going back to her office to give him the space he needs, Zoe tries to get her head back into her work. It won't do itself and she needs to concentrate to get it right.

Half an hour later, Zoe gets a call to bring Laura into Palmer's office.

Less than five minutes later she and a very nervous Laura stand outside Palmer's office door.

"What do I say?" Laura asks Zoe again. "Is he going to sack me? I can't afford to lose my job."

"I don't believe this has anything to do with your job," Zoe tries to assure her, but isn't actually sure that Palmer doesn't plan to do just that. "I think he just wants to know about Conner, the trouble he's in."

"Ok. Wish me luck!" And Laura knocks on the door and enters when Palmer shouts, "Come in."

Try as she might, Zoe can't concentrate on anything. She is far too worried about Laura, Palmer and even Connor.

What has he gotten himself into? If poor Laura loses her job over him, I'll have something to say about it!

Surely Palmer wouldn't penalise Laura over Connor? But she is realising that, no matter how much she loves Palmer, she really doesn't know him that well.

No! I don't believe he would do that! Palmer is a kind person, I may not know him through and through but I know that much!

By the time Laura emerges, crying and sniffling into a tissue, Zoe is half out of her mind.

"Laura! Are you alright?" And Zoe looks past her to where Palmer is standing holding the door open for her. He looks upset, but not angry anymore.

"I'm fine. I just need a minute," Laura tells her, and walks off to the ladies room.

Palmer jerks his head to summon Zoe in to his office.

"You're right," he sighs, "she's head over heels for the idiot. But I think I've managed to find out what's going on."

"Can you stop them from killing him?" Zoe asks, her eyes wide and worried.

"I called a couple of his friends — they say he has been gambling and owes a small time hood named Jennings, a hundred thousand pounds-"

"What!" Zoe shouts, in stunned disbelief.

"I know, it took me back a bit too," Palmer admits. "Now I just have to get in touch with this tough guy, Jennings and pay him off."

"You're just going to hand over a hundred thousand pounds to a stranger you've never met?" Zoe's eyes are all but out on stalks. This just doesn't happen in real life, it has to be some kind of joke!

"I won't be handing anything over until I get Connor's car back," Palmer states. "He can't have it both ways, Zoe — it's the car or the money!"

"But..." She can't think, can't get her mind clear. "Palmer, please, don't get involved. This man could send his goons after you next!"

"If I don't get involved Connor will be dead — Mark was sure about that," he tells her. "I just have to figure a way to get his money to him and get Connor's car back at the same time."

For the rest of the day, Zoe lives on her nerves. She is afraid for Connor, but terrified that Palmer could be getting on the wrong side of a violent criminal.

And what will their mother and father make of it all if it goes horribly wrong? Will they blame me for coming between the brothers, for putting even more distance between them than there already was?

CHAPTER FOURTEEN

For ten years the man standing in Palmer's office has been his friend. But right now, he is being a pain in his rear end!

"Craig, I don't have time to get into this, I want you to run this office if something happens to me," he tells the giant of a man standing over him.

"And I already told you to make the time, because I am not going anywhere until you do!" Craig folds his solid muscle arms across a formidable chest and scowls down at the man who had once been his apprentice on a previous construction company.

He'd taught that boy all he knew, and he'd watched out for him when some of the other guys tried to 'initiate' him into the crew. He wasn't going to stop looking out for him just because he was his boss now and a millionaire to boot!

"Jesus, Craig, you're a stubborn bastard!" Palmer retakes his seat and rings through to Zoe for some coffee, "And something to eat if we have anything available, please."

"Will you just sit! Damn it, Craig, you're giving me a crick in my neck!"

The big man glares down hard, but moves to bring up a chair and drops his considerable weight down onto it.

Palmer tries to glare back at him, but no one does glaring quite as effectively as Big Craig.

"Alright, you win," Palmer smiles and shakes his head. "It's Connor, he's in trouble with a man named Jennings, who kills when a debt isn't paid – and Connor owes him a hundred grand!"

He doesn't explode, doesn't even look surprised, but what Craig does is look angrily at Palmer. "And you thought you would just stroll into his place and pay him off? I thought you had more sense than your brother – it 's not going to happen!"

"Will you stop telling me what you're not going to do – I'm your boss now, remember," Palmer frowns, and still has to look up even with Craig sitting down.

"Yep, that's a fact. Another fact is that I'm your friend – friend trumps boss every damn time!"

A knock at the door has Palmer shouting, "Come in,"

and his temper makes it sound louder than he'd meant.

Instead of Zoe, it is her mother who carries a tray of coffees into the office.

Craig moves quicker than Palmer has ever seen the giant man move before.

"Here, let me take that for you," Craig smiles at Carly Benson and gives her a respectful nod of his head.

Carly actually blushes and smiles back at Craig in an almost girlish, coquettish manner that surprises Palmer.

Remembering herself, Carly turns to Palmer and explains. "I hope you don't mind but, I came in to see Zoe and I heard your request for food with your coffee. I offered to make the drinks while Zoe went out to get you gentlemen something to eat," she tells him. But Carly isn't looking at Palmer now; she is smiling up at Craig.

"That's very kind of you," Craig tells her before Palmer can get a word out. "We really appreciate that."

"Yes, we do," Palmer adds and Carly finally tears her eyes away from Craig and looks over at him.

"I'll leave you gentlemen to your business," Carly smiles and backs out of the room, her eyes back on Craig.

But before they can restart their 'business', another knock comes at the door and Craig springs up to open it.

The big man actually looks crestfallen when he sees that it's Zoe, and not her mother at the door. But he moves back to allow her in with the plates of sandwiches and takes a peak out the door to see if her mother is still around.

When he spots her his smile comes back, brighter than ever and he gives her another polite nod of his head.

"Will you get back over here?!" Palmer asks his foreman with an annoyed frown. And when he retakes his seat, continues, "What the hell is up with you? I've never seen you so much as look at a woman, let alone go gaga over one!"

"That's a fine looking woman," Craig states simply, and keeps his other thoughts to himself.

"Right. So, back to Connor. Where the hell were we?" Palmer asks, struggling to dismiss the image of his foreman fairly drooling over his future mother-in-law.

"We were just discussing us going over to Jennings' place to sort out Connor's mess," Craig says simply. Quiet and determined.

"Damn it, Craig, I don't want to drag you into this," Palmer pushes a distracted hand back through his blond hair and lets out a huge sigh. "But I'm going to say thank you, and just hope that nothing goes wrong!"

"Let's eat," the big man tells his boss. Just that easy, he's pushed his way into bodyguard duty and dropped his heart at a woman's feet. Now it's his stomach that is talking to him, and it is protesting at being empty.

"Who's the man in with Palmer?" Carly asks her daughter when she returns to her desk.

"Oh, that's Craig. He's a giant of a man but apparently there isn't a drop of harm in him," Zoe laughs happily. "Palmer calls him the proverbial 'gentle giant'. I think he's really fond of him. Craig looked after Palmer when he was just an apprentice learning the building trade, and he brought him with him when he started up his own company. Craig didn't hesitate," Zoe states proudly. "Palmer told him what he planned to do and Craig believed in him so much that he gave up a well paid job to help Palmer do it. And he's never regretted it."

"I thought he looked reliable," Carly muses thoughtfully. "And handsome too."

Zoe almost splutters on her coffee. "What did you say?"

"You heard me. I think he's a handsome man, and...so strong," Carly adds quietly, looking back at Palmer's closed office door.

Speechless, Zoe drinks her coffee and eyes her mother warily. Never, in all her born days, has she seen her mother take an interest in a man. It was as if she didn't know they existed, for all the attention she gave them.

But now, Craig of all men. Rough, down to earth,

kindly Craig has caught her eye, and Zoe isn't quite sure what to make of it.

The bar quietens considerably when Palmer and Craig enter it. They order a couple of pints of lager and suss the place out before showing their hand.

"I want to speak to Jennings," Palmer tells the barman, and watches a couple of nearby men come to stand at his back.

Craig does no more than turn to look at the men to have them backing off. But they don't retreat far, and are obviously waiting for orders.

Another man, one bigger than Palmer but nowhere near as big as Craig, walks over to them with a snide grin on his face.

"I think you guys want to move on," the snide man tells them, and a low rumbling chuckle sounds from the rest of the crowd.

"No, I don't think we do." Palmer turns to speak to the man directly. "And if we can't speak to Jennings, then he doesn't get the money I've got for him."

"You give it to me," the man smiles, "and I'll see that the right person gets it."

"Not happening!" Craig's low brown voice growls out.

The snide man pulls himself up to his full height and tries to broaden his chest, but when Craig does the same he puts the man to shame.

"Go and tell your boss we want a word," Palmer moves to Craig's side and raises his brow at the other man. "Or we leave and Jennings is a hundred thousand pounds out of pocket!"

A light goes on over the bar and the snide man frowns up at it.

"Come with me," he tells them, then turns and leads the way to a back room.

"Mr Jennings?" Palmer asks when they face a man in a suite sitting behind a plush office desk in an equally plush office. Not the sort of room they expected to be walking into after the rough looking bar.

"Who wants to know?" the suit asks, his face not showing the slightest emotion.

Christ, this is like playing poker, and with a face like that he'd be a damned good player!

"Connor Johnson – I've come to pay off his debt," Palmer states without giving any more away.

"Then why don't you just hand the money over to my associate – he'll stand you a drink at the bar on your way out," the suit tells them, his face still not cracking a smile, or showing any emotion whatever.

"Because you have a car that belongs to Connor Johnson, and I want it back before I pay you the money he owes you," Palmer states, equally firmly and unrelenting.

The suit looks toward the snide man and nods. But the snide man doesn't look happy.

"But, Mr Jennings, I love that car," the snide man protests. "And you said I could have it."

"Stop whining, Hickey, and do as you're told!" He hadn't raised his voice, but the snide man knew he'd pushed his luck.

When he'd gone, Jennings turns his gaze back to Palmer. "You've got some balls walking in here the way you did. Even with your man there," and he nods towards Craig, "you wouldn't be walking out of here alive if I didn't want you to."

"I'm a business man," Palmer tells him. "As one business man to another, I don't think trouble is what you really want. I have the money you're owed, that's all this is about."

Jennings nods. "True. True. Do you have it with you?"

"I might be green where your kind of business is concerned, but I'm not stupid," Palmer tells him. "I can put my hands on it quick enough – you give me the car back and I'll pay up, only not here. I'll hand it over to Hickey, if you trust him enough, at a public place whenever you say."

Jennings considers, then cracks his face into a chilling smile. "As you say, business. I'll trust you with the car because I know who you are and where to find you. If you don't follow through...I will. Be very certain of that!"

Fuming with Connor for getting him, and Craig, into such a deadly mess, Palmer watches his brother's car being driven by Hickey, pull up in front of him at the kerb.

"You don't pay, I get to have some fun," Hickey sneers, throwing the car keys at Palmer. Then he walks away without a backwards glance, fuming to have lost his status symbol.

"You take my car and I'll drive Connor's," Palmer tells Craig, giving the big man his keys. Then he smiles, "That went better than I expected. I think your presence had an influence," he admits.

"Too damned right!" Craig smiles knowingly. "I'll drive your car back to your office in the morning and pick up a van. Let me know when the drop off is – and don't try to go it alone!"

"Not a chance. You were right, I was glad of your company tonight." Palmer slaps the big man on his arm and gets into Connor's car. Then he drives back to his flat and calls his brother with the good news.

But instead of being grateful, or even just saying thanks, Connor goes off on one big time.

"Why the hell can't you stay out of my business!" Connor tells his brother when Palmer gives him the news.

"I didn't ask you to bail me out. I can take care of myself!"

"Right! Like you did when Hickey beat the shit out of you last weekend!" Palmer tells him, restraining his temper with sheer will alone.

"How the hell do you know about Hickey? Has Laura been shooting her mouth off?"

Just the mention of Laura has Palmer's temper boiling. "If you ever touch that girl again I'll personally kick your arse so hard you won't be able to sit down for a year! And I'm not kidding!"

"You just love playing the big 'I am'," Conner sneers angrily. "Well you can stick your money where the sun doesn't shine, I can take care of my own debts!"

It was tempting, really tempting, to tell Connor that that is just what he will do. But Palmer has given his word and now his and, more importantly, Craig's safety were dependent on him keeping it.

"I'm going to pay Jennings off just as I promised, but you get into any more debt and I'll gladly let you drown in it!" Then Palmer flicks his phone off and throws it across the room in temper.

Blast the man! And I didn't even tell him I got his fucking car back!

CHAPTER FIFTEEN

"So that's what Craig was doing in your office," Zoe guesses, a hand to her worried brow now that Palmer has told her everything. "And you have to meet this man again?"

"Only Hickey, and in broad daylight in a public place," Palmer assures her.

Turning to him, her bottom lip trembling and tears threatening, Zoe winds her arms about his neck and just holds on.

"Hey, hey, it's alright. Nothing happened," Palmer tells her, wrapping his arms about her.

"But it could have," she cries, the tears falling freely now. "I could have lost you, and you and Craig could have been found in some alley, dead."

Just hearing the thought out loud makes Palmer

shudder, and he holds Zoe tighter to him. "Shush, now. I'm fine and Craig's fine — nothing happened. Nothing happened," he tells her again, and waits for her sobs to ease.

"Getting back to Craig," Palmer tries to distract Zoe by changing the subject, "I think he has a thing for your mother!"

Chuckling, Zoe dries her eyes and blows her nose, then looks up at Palmer. "I think my mother has a 'thing' for Craig too. I've never seen her like that over a man. Usually she doesn't even notice them."

"Craig too," Palmer confirms. "I think we should invite them both over to dinner at my place. Perhaps we should invite my mum and dad just to make it less obvious," he adds with a laugh.

"I don't think subtlety will come into it. But I do think it would be nice to have your parent's there too. When do you think we should arrange this little dinner party?" Zoe laughs, feeling the weight of her recent worries lifting finally.

"Let's wait until this business with Connor is taken care of, then we can enjoy ourselves more," Palmer suggests, and kisses Zoe lightly on the lips.

"Ok, but no heroics — you make sure Craig is with you and you come back safe! I do not want to be a widow before I even have the chance to get married!" she frowns, and he feels the shudder run through her slight body.

"Not a chance! And talking of weddings, when are we planning to get married?" he asks, tipping his head to one side and smiling warmly.

"I haven't a clue – did you have any thoughts on the timing?"

"Depends, do you want a summer or a Christmas wedding?"

"Palmer! Are you talking about this year?" Zoe asks, stunned and panicking.

"Of course this year," Palmer laughs, and picks her up, twirling her around.

Laughing, Zoe holds on to Palmer. "But summer has already started, it'll have to be a Christmas wedding," she grins.

When he lowers her down his body, Palmer keeps her close. "I want to make you my wife as soon as possible – but Christmas it is if that's your wish."

"Oh my goodness, setting a date makes it so real," Zoe blinks, and looks at Palmer with a whole new set of worries in her eyes. "Now I need to start planning!"

"Then get to it woman!" And Palmer releases her, giving her backside a firm slap.

Later that evening, Palmer and Craig go to the Bullring Shopping Centre. Hickey is already there with a couple of goons standing next to him.

"Make sure that gets to Jennings!" Palmer hands over a bag containing the cash as agreed.

Hickey takes the bag and sniggers at Palmer and Craig. "Tell your brother I'll be seeing him again soon, he'll never stop gambling!"

"Don't bet on it!" Palmer tells him, and Craig lets out a long rumbling laugh.

With the deal done, and Connor's arse saved for another day, Palmer and Craig go back to the car.

"What are you gonna do about Connor?"

"I don't know, but I've got to think of a way of keeping him away from the likes of Jennings and Hickey!"

"Give him to me," Craig's deep voice demands sternly. "The Italian job will be starting in a week – I'll take him with me and work him till he sees sense!"

Frowning, Palmer considers his old friend's suggestion. "It would get him away for a while, and with you watching him he might actually come out of this a better man."

"I'll keep him close for the next week. He'll be too tired to play around after work!" Craig promises.

By the time Palmer gets back to his loft apartment, he

is feeling much more positive about his concerns over Connor.

"All done," he tells Zoe, who has prepared an evening meal for them both. "And Craig is going to take Connor very firmly under his wing. He's going to take him to Italy for the Rodriguez job at the end of next week."

"Next week! That doesn't give us long to get the dinner party together," Zoe tells him, eyes wide and letting out a huge sigh.

Pushing a hand back through his hair, Palmer admits that he'd forgotten about it. "Not the best timing, but we can pull it in. How about Friday?"

"You phone your parents and I'll phone my mother." Zoe picks up her mobile and shoos Palmer off to do the same. When they both get off their phones the arrangements are made. "Now you just have to get Craig here," she reminds him.

"Hmm, that could be tricky. He isn't the sociable type, and I'm not sure whether to tell him your mother will be here or not?"

"I thought you said he likes her?" Zoe frowns, thinking of her mother's reaction to Craig earlier that day.

"No doubt about it. He was bowled over. It's just, a dinner party isn't really his thing — but I'll work my way around it somehow."

When Connor hears what Palmer and Craig have done, he goes ballistic.

"Who the hell does he think he is?!" Connor rages, pacing up and down the site port-a-cabin. "And why the fuck did he involve you? My life is no concern of either of you!"

"That's where you're wrong!" Craig gets up from behind his desk and moves to tower over Connor. "You will be working with me from now on. You will do what I say when I say, and I don't want to hear any back-chat while you're doing it!"

Although Connor doesn't give any ground, he has the sense not to argue outright. "He can't make me do anything I don't want to," Connor protests, not challenging Craig directly. "I work for him, he doesn't own me!"

Taking just one more step, Craig brings himself to stand toe-to-toe with Connor. "Your brother just saved your life – make no mistake about that. I was there, I saw the way things were going, and your funeral was definitely on the cards!"

"Shit!" Connor spins around and walks away from the big foreman. "It still wasn't any of his business!"

"One day, when you're all grown up, you might have

the balls to thank him!" Craig returns to his seat and just looks at Connor with ice in his eyes. "Till then, you're mine. You'll work off your debt by getting your hands dirty and the jobs done! And at the end of the week we leave for Italy!"

"Italy! You have got to be fucking joking. I've got plans, I've-"

"What you've got..." Craig interrupts Connor's tirade with impunity, "...is a responsibility that you will honour! If I have to kick your skinny arse all over this building site and across to Italy, then be assured, I will do so!"

Glaring now, knowing that he has no choice, Connor turns to storm out. "I'll go, but not because I owe Palmer anything! I didn't ask him to bail me out; it was none of his damned business!"

Watching the young man slam out of the port-a-cabin, Craig sits shaking his head.

How can two brothers be so different? One the salt-of-the-earth, the other heading for hell in a heartbeat if he isn't careful!

Connor picks up his tool belt and starts hammering seven bells out of a piece of wood that he is fitting into a stud wall frame.

His anger is so hot and deep, he vows to pay Palmer back for what he sees as a public humiliation. At 24, he is still young enough to act rashly, and sees his brother as the bane of his existence.

If Palmer wants me to take on more of the business, then I will. If my brother wants me to get more involved with family and friends, I will. Until I'm good and ready to do exactly what I wants to do! Then Palmer will know what it's like to suffer instead of getting everything handed to him on a damned plate!

Just wait and see, bro, even Zoe will choose me when I'm done with you and yours!

The first arrivals for the dinner party are due in a little over an hour. Zoe lays Palmer's dining table with a centre flower arrangement and his best place-mats and cutlery. "Where are your wine glasses?" she shouts to Palmer, who is just now exiting the shower.

He walks out of the bathroom with a towel slung around his hips and walks over to hug her from behind.

Bringing his lips to her neck, Palmer breathes in the scent of his fiancé and wishes they had time for more than just a hug.

"You know, this dinner party is all set – you've done a great job," he tells her, while his teeth nibble gently on her ear. "Maybe we should take the time for some really hot sex to relax us," and his hands push her robe aside and move up to cup a pair of warm naked breasts.

"Palmer...oh lordy..." she breathes, her head falling back onto his shoulder. "We...we don't have time."

But he can feel her body relaxing against his and knows that he can convince her to make time.

The last week has been fraught with tension at work and family worries. Now those tensions are falling away and Palmer can think of nothing better than having his woman in his arms...and his bed.

One good thing about loft living, is that everything is in the same room – even the bed.

Just a couple more steps. Turning her in his arms, Palmer kisses her so thoroughly that Zoe can't tell what day it is, let alone keep an eye on the time.

Before she knows it, her hands are in his hair and she's kissing him back with all the hunger of new love.

The bed catches the backs of her legs and Zoe tumbles on to it with Palmer following. His breathing is ragged, matched by her growing pants of arousal.

"Palmer, we can't do this," she protests, but opens to him at the same time.

"Relax, baby, and just let me love you," he whispers, his mouth now traversing her belly and moving lower.

A loud groan tells him he is winning, and Palmer soon moves over her for the victory dance.

Once, twice, he pushes into her, slowly, deeply, taking

his time to draw out the growing ache in their joined loins.

But it's Zoe who clutches his buttocks, pulling him to her eagerly, needing him to fill her and take her to peak.

She isn't thinking of the dinner party now, or the fact that her mother is due to be the first to arrive. All Zoe knows now is the touch and feel of Palmer, and the love he brings to her.

Her thighs tighten around him, and Palmer can feel her whole body tense.

Now he isn't so gentle, not holding back he plunges fast and hard and Zoe screams for more.

"Palmer!" Just his name, but it sounds so sweet when caught up in the throes of passion that he wants to hear it again.

Pushing her legs back, he raises himself to his knees and withdraws almost fully, then takes her with a force that leaves her gasping.

Her first peak is high and fast, but her second builds from somewhere deep inside of her and answers to Palmer's demanding thrusts.

"Now, Zoe! Now!"

She shudders violently, tightening around him until he has no choice but to follow her lead and empties into her.

So wonderful. So completely and utterly wonderful.

Their loving has been less frequent of late, but now they have certainly made up for it.

"Sorry if I've put you behind with dinner," he tells her, not really sorry at all. "But I just couldn't keep my hands off you. I love you so much, Zoe Benson, and I can't wait to make you my wife!"

Smiling like a cat that just devoured a pitcher of top quality cream, Zoe snuggles deep into Palmer's arms and purrs. "I'm not complaining, though I will need to get up soon. Just...not quite yet," she moans, her leg moving over to tangle with his, her lips grazing his chest as she tastes the heat of passion still covering his well toned body.

Ten minutes later, it's Palmer who has to encourage Zoe to get up. "If we don't get up now I'll end up in the dog-house when your mother arrives and you aren't ready!"

She groans but nods, "You're right, of course. I just love the way sex makes me feel — all relaxed and loose and lazy as hell."

"Me too. Whose bright idea was this dinner party anyway?!"

CHAPTER SIXTEEN

Dressed and ready for their first guest to arrive, Zoe and Palmer enjoy a pre-dinner glass of wine.

"Here's to our first official dinner party as a couple," Zoe clinks glasses with Palmer and smiles broadly at him.

"The first of many." Palmer returns her smile and places a quick kiss on her lips before crossing to answer the door.

"Mrs Benson," he greets Zoe's mother, "please come in."

"Mum," Zoe embraces her mother and draws her further into the lounge area of Palmer's loft apartment.

"This...is...different," Carly Benson observes, turning in a slow circle to take in the unusual layout of the flat.

"Isn't it lovely?" Zoe enthuses. "It's so spacious, and at night the views are spectacular!"

Moving to the tall windows, Carly looks out over the still busy city. "I imagine it's beautiful when the city lights come on."

Another knock and Palmer once again crosses to admit a dinner guest. "Hi Laura, Connor, glad you decided to come."

"Sure, why not," Connor mutters, and walks straight over to Palmer's supply of whiskey to help himself to a glass.

"Hey, Laura," Zoe greets her friend and work colleague.

"Hi, Zoe, thanks for asking us over," Laura grins as she follows her further into the room. "Oh my god, this is amazing," Laura turns as Carly had and stares at her surroundings open mouthed.

"It is pretty great," Zoe agrees.

When the door is knocked again, Zoe returns to it and greets Palmer's parents, and Craig!

"Come in," she grins, amazed that Palmer actually managed to talk his foreman into coming to dinner. "Dorothy, Bill, it's good to see you. And you too, Craig," she beams up at the gentle giant.

"I brought these," Craig tells her, handing her a bunch of flowers, "and this."

"Wine and flowers," Dorothy gives a nod of approval,

"you're mother brought you up right!"

Craig actually blushes, but has to pull himself together quickly when he spots Carly Benson on the opposite side of the room.

"Come on in and sit down," Palmer invites, waving over to his seating area.

Drinks are dispensed to all and the conversation flows easily. Even Craig and Carly are chatting away with surprising ease.

"Palmer, if you could just help me to set the dinnerware on the table, we can start eating," Zoe turns and tells the assembled company.

The dining table has been extended to seat eight comfortably. Palmer sits at one end with Zoe on his right and her mother on his left. Next to Carly is Craig and then Laura, with Connor at the opposite end to Palmer and then his mother Dorothy and his father Bill.

The meal is a roaring success. Even Connor appears to get into the spirit of things, conversing easily with his parents and all the other guests.

But there is still tension between the brother's. Both seem to steer clear of any actual direct conversation, which suits Zoe just fine.

By the time desert is finished and at least four bottles of wine drunk, most people are feeling comfortable and easy with the company around them.

Connor, however, decides he's done his duty and urges Laura to follow suit when he says that he has to leave.

"Goodnight, mother, father, I'll see you back at home later," he tells them. "That was...interesting," Connor smiles at Zoe and gives his brother a brief nod. "See you at work, Craig. Goodnight, Mrs Benson."

Then he and Laura take their leave and the atmosphere is strained for a brief while.

"He is always on the go with something," Dorothy offers and smiles at Carly and Craig. "Don't know where the young get their energy; I don't remember being able to burn the candle at both ends the way Connor does!"

"He'll be needing to get some rest tomorrow," Craig tells her. "We fly out to Sorrento in Italy tomorrow night."

Turning to Palmer, Dorothy frowns. "Why on earth hasn't he mentioned it? I know nothing of Connor going to Italy!"

"Stop fretting," Bill Johnson pats his wife's hand. "The boy doesn't tell you half of what he gets up to, and be glad of it or you'd worry yourself into an early grave!"

"That is not a comforting thought!" Dorothy tells her husband.

But truer words were never spoken!

"I'll watch out for him, Mrs Johnson," Craig smiles reassuringly. "We'll have our work cut out with the hotel we're going to be renovating, so it won't leave a lot of time for him to get into any trouble."

"How long do you expect to be away?" Carly asks with keen interest.

"About six weeks to two months, depending on how straightforward or complicated the job is," Craig explains.

"Oh, I see," Carly looks a little crestfallen. "That's quite a little while; won't your family miss you?"

"I don't have any family," Craig tells her softly. "My parents both died years ago and I've never been married, so it's just me."

"Oh," Carly smiles, but inside her heart leaps.

"Why don't you show Craig the view, mother?" Zoe suggests. "It's quite dark and the city lights are coming on."

Watching her mother and Craig cross the room together, Zoe turns to Palmer and grins.

"You two are playing cupid," Dorothy observes quietly. "And I must say, it seems to be working."

Craig and Carly are totally absorbed in each other. Neither is now aware of the company they moved away from.

"It would be nice for your mother to have someone in

her life after so long," Dorothy tells Zoe. "And it's nice to see that you are encouraging her to meet someone. Children can be jealous of a parent taking up with someone new."

Grimacing, Zoe has to admit the reason she wants her mother to meet someone. "It's better than thinking of her being alone once Palmer and I get married. Which won't be long, if your son has his way," Zoe tells her.

"You can't go rushing into this," Dorothy tells her son and future daughter-in-law.

"Christmas, mother, and not a day later!" Palmer insists.

"Leave them to it," Bill warns his wife. "It's none of our business. And besides...," he grins, "...the sooner they get married the sooner we get our grandchildren!"

Brightening considerable, Dorothy says, "True. True. How long do you think you'll leave it before you start trying?"

Zoe blushes furiously, her cheeks hot enough to fry an egg on.

"Give us a chance to enjoy being married first," Palmer warns.

"So, have you set the date?" Dorothy asks, then looks up as Carly and Craig return to the seating area.

"Set the date for what?" Carly asks.

"For the wedding," Bill grins.

"You never said anything," Carly complains, looking from her daughter to Palmer and back again.

"We haven't actually set a date properly," Palmer interjects, casting his parents a reproving look. "We talked earlier about a Christmas wedding, but nothing firm has been decided."

"Well, I suppose it would be doable, but we'd have to get our skates on," Carly warns, smiling now at her daughter.

"Do you really think so?" Zoe beams, and the talk now focuses on wedding plans.

The following day, Palmer helps at the construction yard to get the men together and transport them all to the airport. He takes three and their suitcases in his car and Zoe takes the same in hers.

"Don't wait to get in touch if you hit any problems," Palmer tells Craig. "I know you know what you're doing, but I'll be worrying anyway. Especially about the problem you're taking with you," he states cryptically.

"That won't be a problem for long. I'll soon work the rough edges off him and fatigue will do the rest," Craig assures him.

For the rest of their weekend, Zoe and Palmer relax at his flat and enjoy some time together.

Life feels pretty darn good. The Connor problem seems to have been resolved without any comeback. Nothing has been heard from Hickey or Jennings since the payoff.

And the man himself is now on his way to Italy and will be gone for around six beautiful weeks.

"So, where do you think our wedding should be held?" Palmer asks Zoe as she lies in his arms as they watch TV.

"I don't have a clue – I thought you would know more about that," she tells him, looking up at Palmer wide-eyed.

"Hmm, I'll give it some thought. Even though mum and dad's cottage has a lot of land, it would be a bit cold for a marquee at Christmas."

Nodding, Zoe has to agree. "Yep, indoors does sound more sensible. But would it have to be a church?"

"I'm easy about that if you are. Perhaps a smart hotel or small country house," Palmer suggests. Then he laughs and pulls her into him. "I can't believe we're planning our wedding – I'm actually excited about it all!"

"Me too," Zoe laughs. "I'm going to need to start thinking about the colours I want – the bouquets, the men's cravats and suits, the bridesmaid's dresses and the corsages."

"You seem to have forgotten about your wedding dress," Palmer points out.

"Not in the least, but I can't talk about that with you. It wouldn't be right," she tells him firmly. "I'll be discussing that with my mother and probably Laura. I'm hoping she will be one of my bridesmaids."

"Is that because you've become good friends, or are you trying to include Connor somehow?"

"A bit of both," Zoe admits. "Will you ask him to be your best-man?"

"Depends. If he comes through in Italy and doesn't mess up again, then yes, I'd be happy to ask him," Palmer concedes. "But if he does mess up again, I won't trust him enough to do it. Then I'll ask Craig – he's one of the oldest and best friends I've got. It would be an honour to have him stand with me."

CHAPTER SEVENTEEN

At work the following Monday, Zoe tells Laura all about the wedding talk and their plans to have a Christmas wedding.

"I think we'll probably get married the weekend before, so that we'll be on honeymoon over Christmas itself," Zoe muses aloud.

"And what about the honeymoon, where do you think you'll go?" Laura asks, getting into the spirit of the discussion. "I've always thought it would be nice to go somewhere tropical, like one of those island paradises that you see on the television."

They laugh, and their suggestions become more and more outlandish.

"Ok, I've got one – how about the first honeymoon in space," Laura laughs loudly. "Can you imagine the sex;

you'd be literally floating around, hanging from the ceiling if you wanted to!"

"I'm not sure that would work," Zoe giggles at the improbable thought. "But a honeymoon on board a private yacht would be amazing. Imagine being able to go where you want when you want, and topless sunbathing on deck with no one around to see you!"

"Hmm, what about the crew?" Laura raises an eyebrow. "Unless you and Palmer are planning to do it all yourselves, which won't actually leave much time for sunbathing – or anything else, come to that!"

"Ok, scratch that, I'll have to give it some more thought," Zoe grins happily.

"So, where are you planning to get married – will it be a church wedding?" Laura frowns, trying to think whether she's ever heard Connor mention the family going to church.

"We were thinking of a small manor house type venue – but neither of us knows of anywhere," Zoe admits. "I think we'll end up trawling the internet for local venues, or somewhere not too far out of the way at least."

At the end of a very long day, having not seen Palmer in the office all day, Zoe locks up and goes down to her car.

An envelope, pinned under the wiper blade on the

driver's side of the car, has her name on it.

What the heck? Why would anyone leave a note addressed to me on my car?

Ripping it open, Zoe's happy balloon bursts with a debilitating pop.

"No, this can't be real – someone is playing a nasty trick on me!" But she can't stop reading the words over and over again. 'Keep your hands off Palmer. He's mine!'

Zoe walks slowly across the car park to the builder's yard at the back of the building. Most of the vans are parked and locked up, and she can't see anyone else around through the locked metal gate.

But she feels like she is being watched. Otherwise how did this someone know which car to put the note on?

Hers is the last car in the car park; even the cars belonging to the other businesses that lease space in the building are all gone.

Walking back to it, Zoe checks the back seats before climbing into her car.

She'd read that tip somewhere and now the relevance of it makes her spine tingle and her heart race.

Starting the car she begins heading home, but a nagging thought makes her turn the car around and head over to Palmer's flat.

He isn't expecting her. *But he won't mind me just dropping by – will he?*

Pulling up next to Palmer's car, Zoe locks hers and heads for the lift lobby.

This can't be real...he's never mentioned anyone that he's recently finished with! Unless...he hasn't finished with her...

No. No. No. I won't start doubting him just because some nut puts a letter on my car! And what does 'he's mine' mean anyway – you can't own another person?!

But when the lift reaches the top floor – Palmer's floor – Zoe steps out of the lift and stands looking at his front door.

Will he be angry that I came here? Will it look like I'm accusing him of being unfaithful? Maybe I should just leave before he knows I'm here?

But what about the note? Someone put a note specifically addressed to me on my car. That means they know me and my car and where I work!

Holy shit! Someone is stalking me! Maybe they even know where I live!

There is nothing else for it, Zoe reaches out and presses the bell on Palmer's front door and hops from foot to foot while she waits for him to answer.

"Zoe," he smiles brightly, "I didn't expect to see you tonight. Is everything alright? Was work ok?"

"Work was fine. I even heard from Craig about the

Rodriguez Hotel. He said it's all going well – the building is a lot stronger than it first looked, apparently."

Unable to help herself, Zoe finds herself looking around for signs that Palmer has had someone else over.

"This was pinned under my windscreen wiper when I knocked off work tonight." There, she had said it, and she hands him the envelope with the brief letter inside.

Palmer's smile slips and a frown puckers his brow. "You want me to read it?"

"You can, or I can tell you what it says – it's very succinct. It says, 'Keep your hands off Palmer. He's mine!'" Then she turns to look at him, her eyes filled with hurt. "Any ideas?" Zoe asks, and he knows exactly what she means.

"You think this is from a woman I've been seeing behind your back?" he asks, his voice low and edged with restrained anger.

"I think someone went to a lot of trouble to put that on my car at the place where I work," Zoe states, her voice flat and void of any emotion.

"Zoe...this is crazy...I am not cheating on you and I'm not thrilled that you think me capable of such deceit!"

"I haven't accused you of anything, but I would like some sort of explanation," she murmurs, with just a slight tremor as she turns away from Palmer and walks to look out of the window.

Is she out there? Did she watch me come in here knowing what I'd do?

"Zoe..." his voice is soft and has a plea in it now, "...you have to believe me, I have no idea what this note means or who might have sent it. You do believe me, right?"

When his hands touch her shoulders, Zoe has to steady herself not to pull away. "Then, I can only assume that I'm being stalked by someone with an ulterior motive – a scary thought, I don't mind admitting."

Turning her, Palmer looks down into her troubled brown eyes. Not the usual pools of happiness or the mirrors of passion that he has so often looked into. She is afraid, and with good reason.

"Move in here with me," he suggests. "We can go to work together and I'll make sure to be there at the end of day to take you home. No one will get to you while I'm around!"

This is crazy! Zoe Benson you are being totally unreasonable! One stupid letter and you go to pieces!

"No, I won't let some idiotic note make me run for cover. And that's what I'd be doing if I moved in with you now," she admits. "When we move in together it will be because it's what we decide, what we want – not in response to someone's idea of a sick joke!"

Pulling her into his arms, Palmer holds her tight against him. "Zoe, I don't care about anyone else — I care about keeping you safe!"

"You think maybe I'm in danger?" she asks, her head tipped back to look up at him, her eyes wide with alarm.

"I think I don't like the way this happened. And If I didn't know that Connor was in Italy, I might think it was down to him."

"But that's ridiculous! What possible reason could Connor have for trying to split us up?"

"I've lived with his unreasoned jealously for all of Connor's life," Palmer tells her firmly. "I mean it, Zoe. Connor has never needed a reason to be jealous other than I have something that he hasn't.

It started with birthday and Christmas presents but it soon moved on to bigger things, like friends and even girlfriends," Palmer explains, moving them to sit on a settee. "Zoe, I know how it sounds, I've been through something like this before. Only then it wasn't so subtle, or impossible to prove."

Shaking her head, Zoe looks at Palmer like he's telling her a tall tale that makes no sense.

"When I was 21 I met a girl I fell for pretty heavily." Palmer gets up and begins to pace around the seating area of his loft.

"It sounded just as petty and unlikely then too, but I knew Connor was at the back of that breakup too. And guess who her new boyfriend was within weeks of us ending," he looks back at Zoe and nods. "Yes, you've guessed it, Mr Connor Johnson. But it didn't last. Because as with everything else that I had and Connor wanted, once she was his he lost interest and the fun of taunting me soon wore off."

"You make him sound crazy," Zoe laughs nervously.

"No, not crazy, and not in the least bit unwitting," Palmer states vehemently.

"Actually, I really don't find that to be as comforting as you might have meant it to be," Zoe frowns up at her still pacing fiancé. "I mean, to think that he would deliberately want to sabotage your relationships is one thing, but to think he would plan something like this from as far away as Italy just makes him plain scary!"

"It may not be Connor," Palmer comes to sit beside Zoe and takes her hand. "But if it is, I'm going to find out who is helping him and how!"

"And if it isn't...?"

"Then someone is in for an unpleasant surprise. I intend to find out who they are and confront them," Palmer asserts. "They can't hide forever."

"But what do I do until they are caught?"

"I've told you, you move in with me and let me watch everyone you come into contact with – even at work," Palmer says, his face now set with determination. "I want to know who you speak to on the phone or in the office each day, anything they say that might make you uncomfortable or suggest they know more about your movements than they should. Then I'll set a tail on them, I'll look into anyone you come into contact with until they have nowhere left to hide!"

It sounds like a plan, but it also sounds like a virtual cage. But if that's what it takes to catch this creep, maybe it will be worth it!

"Ok. We'll try it your way and see what happens. But I'll need to go home to pack a few things, even just for the next few days," she tells him with a tremulous smile.

"No problem, I'll take you now and then we'll go out for dinner," Palmer suggests more positively.

"Oh lordy, dinner! My mother will have cooked already, she's expecting me home." Pulling her mobile out of her bag, Zoe calls home to let her mother know where she is. "I'm sorry mum, I just didn't think. But if there's enough for three Palmer could stay for dinner too." Listening as her mother tells her how worried she's been, thinking her daughter might have been in a traffic accident, Zoe tries not to wince.

"Ok, ok, we'll be there in about twenty minutes if we leave now," Zoe says, hoping her mother will relent, and when she does, Zoe smiles thankfully up at Palmer. "Ok, mum, we'll see you soon."

Sagging forward, Zoe rests her forehead onto Palmers arm.

"I gather your mother wasn't exactly pleased to be receiving an unexpected dinner guest," he laughs softly.

"No, you're very welcome," she tells him. "It's me that's in the doghouse for not thinking to ring her before this and causing her to worry. But she'll be fine by the time we get there. And we'd better put our skates on; it wouldn't do to keep her waiting a second time!"

CHAPTER EIGHTEEN

Moving in with Palmer hadn't been the easy solution that Zoe had hoped for. Her mother had protested vehemently, but Zoe hadn't wanted to explain the extraneous circumstances that had lead to their decision. That would have worried her mother even more.

And so they had played up the love angle, saying that they didn't want to wait until Christmas to live together.

Eventually her mother had relented, even wishing them well and giving them a treasured crystal vase to mark the day.

An unofficial housewarming present, she had called it. But as much as she had tried to smile, Zoe had known that her mother wasn't truly happy to see her daughter leave the nest.

"I wish Craig were back," Zoe murmurs as she sits on

the settee with Palmer watching the television. "He seemed really interested in my mother, and I hate to think of her alone."

It has been a week since she left home, and Zoe is brooding and uneasy.

Yes it has been wonderful to wake up next to Palmer each morning, to do all the everyday things together. But it still doesn't feel right.

Nothing has happened since moving in with Palmer, and that was, of course, the plan. But now she wonders if they have been hasty.

"You want to move back home," Palmer states rather than asks. "But how will things be different when we're married?"

"Well, maybe Craig and my mother will hit it off and start seeing each other," Zoe suggests hopefully.

"And if they don't, do we have to wait for your mother to meet someone before you can be happy for us to live together? That's a big ask considering she's been alone for so many years," he adds sagely.

"No, I suppose not," Zoe murmurs, feeling childish and unreasonable. "It's just, when we get married moving out will be a natural progression – this way, I just decided to leave home, to leave her all alone."

Sighing, Palmer tries to sooth her worries, but knows Zoe isn't comfortable with things as they are.

The following morning, they go down to the parking area together, and walk over to Palmer's car for him to drop her off at work, as he has done every day that week.

"Look," Zoe's eyes watch as an envelope flaps in the breeze, pinned beneath her windscreen wiper as before.

But before she can reach it, Palmer walks to her car and takes the envelope.

He rips it open having first read her name on the front of it. "Damn it! This is going beyond a joke!"

"Let me see," Zoe holds her hand out for the letter. But Palmer has already shoved it into his pocket.

"You don't need to read that rubbish," he growls out, opening his car and climbing in behind the wheel.

Zoe stands watching him, stunned by Palmer's behaviour.

Having climbed in the passenger side, Zoe doesn't clip her seatbelt on but sits looking at Palmer expectantly.

"You don't need to read the kind of lies they've written about me," he tells her, and turns the ignition key to start the car.

But Zoe still doesn't move, "I'd like to know what I'm up against if nothing else. The letter please, Palmer," and she holds her hand out towards him.

"Damn it, Zoe!" But he reaches into his pocket and hands her the letter.

Looking at her name printed on the front of the envelope she says, "Same handwriting." Pulling the letter out it doesn't take long to read. "As succinct as the other one too, just 'you're not the first'. So what does that mean?" Zoe asks, her voice as unemotional as her expression.

"I don't know what it means," Palmer turns away from her and prepares to reverse out of the parking space. "Put your seatbelt on, Zoe. We're going to be late."

This time she does buckle up, but Zoe can't let it alone.

"You must have some idea, or you wouldn't have called it lies," she reminds him.

"It's obvious that it is implying that I've been unfaithful to you and that it isn't the first time," he grates out angrily. "But it isn't true – I've never been deceitful in any of my relationships, and I'm not being unfaithful to you now, damn it!"

"I believe you," she tells him simply, and hears his whoosh of relief.

"Well thank heavens for that! But why, you've only got my word for it?"

"Your word is good enough," she tells him. "I don't believe I could love a man capable of such duplicity. I've always had good instincts about people, and I knew I liked you from the minute you saved me from falling flat on my face when I fell out of the lift!"

Laughing with relief, Palmer turns off the engine, unbuckles his seatbelt and just pulls her into his arms.

"I have never loved anyone as thoroughly as I love you," he tells her, his voice dripping with emotion. "When I saw that letter I knew it had to be bad, and it scared the hell out of me to think you might believe their lies. Whoever 'they' are."

Laying a gentle hand against his cheek, Zoe looks deep into his glittering blue eyes. The emotion she can see there has to be real, no one could fake that.

"I love you, too. We'll find out what's going on but in the meantime, we just have to believe in each other...trust each other, Palmer."

His eyelids fall, hiding the moisture gathering beneath them.

"I love you, Zoe. I love you so much it scares me, even without this mess to harass us." Holding her, Palmer needs to feel her safe in his arms and silently vows to find whoever is responsible for trying to put doubts between them.

She doesn't move back home, but neither do the letters stop coming. Now they are arriving at work, through the post, pushed through the letter box, or pinned under her windscreen wiper.

And just when she doesn't think things can get much worse, her mother calls her at work.

"Hi, Zoe, will you be coming by this evening?" her mother asks, and as it is Friday this isn't unusual in itself. But she has never before rung Zoe at work to confirm their usual routine.

"Of course mum, unless you need to cancel."

"No. No, I just wanted to be sure as there's a letter here for you. It's a bit unusual," Carly observes, distractedly turning the envelope over in her hands, "it appears to have been hand delivered – at least, I can't see any postmark on it."

"I see," Zoe says quietly, trying not to think the worst but feeling a gnawing dread in the pit of her stomach.

"Zoe, I know that tone – what is going on?" her mother demands.

"It's nothing, just a prank that has become tiresome," she tries to dismiss the incident as nothing more than a mild irritation, but fails pitifully.

"Don't lie to me, Zoe Benson. I know when my own daughter is worried," Carly tells her firmly.

Fear, dread and unthinkable doubts begin to cloud Zoe's judgement. The letters have become relentless and their insinuations more blatantly accusing.

"I'm fine, mum. But maybe we could talk tonight," she

tells her, and knows that she will tell her mother everything, despite her agreement with Palmer not to speak of it with anyone.

"Alright, Zoe," her mother agrees, knowing that right now is not the time to push her daughter. "Do you want me to keep this letter...or should I burn it?"

From her tone, it is obvious to Zoe that her mother has guessed that the letter is the root of her despondency.

"Burn it," she replies instinctively, then changes her mind. "No, don't, I need to see what it says...even if I don't believe it."

The line goes silent, both women contemplating what has been left unsaid.

"I'll have your dinner waiting for you," Carly tells her, deciding that there is nothing more to be said for the moment. "Just put your mind into your work and let the rest wait."

Then she is gone and Zoe is left to do as her mother suggested. But it isn't easy, and her mind struggles to stay focused.

Walking out to her car, Zoe is relieved not to find another letter pinned to her windscreen, then remembers the one waiting for her at her mother's house.

How the hell did they know to post it there? They not

only know my old address but may also have known that I would be visiting this evening?

That means they're following me! Whoever they are, they are tracking my every move somehow!

The thought scares the living hell out of her, and not for the first time Zoe thought about going to the police.

But Palmer had been reluctant to go down that route, preferring to keep the nature of the letters private.

I can understand that. I wouldn't want the police poking into my private affairs. Affairs...what an odd word with such different meanings...

By the time she reaches her mother's house, Zoe is tensed up to breaking point.

The strain is beginning to show and she has to calm her breathing before walking to the front door.

Her mum opens it even before she has a chance to knock, and when she sees Zoe simply draws her in and closes the door.

"Oh, mum." The flood gates open, and nothing can hold back the tide of emotion that flows out with the tears.

Taking her daughter into the sitting room, Carly leads her to a settee and just holds her until the worst is over.

Handing her a bunch of tissues, Carly draws back to look at her daughter and doesn't like what she sees.

Taking the envelope out of her pocket, Carly hands it to her daughter and watches her response. The nervous frown tells its own tale, and Carly prepares to hear the worst.

Opening the letter, Zoe reads the brief note and crumples it in her hands, letting them fall into her lap.

"I can't take this much more," Zoe declares. "This poison is so relentless. No matter what I do I can't get it out of my mind. And Poor Palmer is suffering too, so very much."

"May I read it?" Carly asks quietly.

At first Zoe is reluctant, but hands it over to her mother.

She watches her mother read the words over and over, then her eyes level with Zoe's.

"And you're sure this is lies," her mother asks, her face giving nothing away.

"It has to be," Zoe protests. "I can't believe that Palmer would be so callous. To say that he has a bastard child that he doesn't care about is preposterous. Palmer loves children, he can't wait until we have our own – he told me so," she protests harder, not sure who she is trying to convince.

"Have the other letters been along the same vein?" Carly asks.

"How do you know there have been others?" Zoe asks, stumped as always by her seemingly omniscient mother.

"It would make sense to work up to such an accusation," Carly explains. "How many others have there been?"

"This is the thirteenth." Zoe rubs her forehead, trying to relieve the headache that is growing fast.

"Have you kept them?"

She wants to say no, that she has tossed them away without a care, but she can't.

"Yes. I don't know why, but I just stuffed them in a drawer at work," she says instead.

"Ok. Well, let's eat. I always think best when I'm not hungry," Carly smiles, trying to lighten the mood, and is grateful when her daughter responds in kind.

They talk about all manner of things, but save the main topic for after their meal.

"The hotel in Italy appears to be going well," Zoe states more happily. "According to Craig they'll be finished at least a week before they anticipated."

"Yes, he said they hoped to be back by the end of next week," Carly replies, surprising her daughter with a fork full of food stopped halfway to her mouth. "What! I can't have a telephone conversation with a man?"

"I...no...I mean...when did you start receiving calls from Craig?" Zoe splutters, nonplussed by her mother's revelation.

"Since we met at dinner at Palmer's flat," Carly states nonchalantly. "He's very sweet."

Sweet! I'll bet Craig would cringe at being described as 'sweet'. That title doesn't exactly match his build and rough exterior. But if my mother thinks he's sweet, then sweet is what he is!

"Are you going to see each other when he gets back?" Zoe asks, not really comfortable talking about her mother possibly dating someone.

"We've talked about it. Why, would it bother you if I did?" Carly asks.

"No. Not in the least," Zoe assures her. "You've never spoken much about dad, but I'm glad you're getting over whatever happened. I'd like to see you happy with someone." And having said it, Zoe realises that it is true and smiles brightly at her mother.

"Your father hurt me deeply, I loved him so much that his infidelity cut me to the quick," Carly recalls. "It didn't help that I was still carrying some extra weight from having you and the very young woman he left me for was so beautiful and slim. I felt I'd let myself down and lost him because of it."

"But you know that wasn't so?" Zoe frowns, hoping that her mother hasn't been carrying such a negative image of herself around for all these years.

"Oh, I know that now," Carly assures her. "But it took a long time to regain my self-esteem. And by the time I did, it didn't really matter. I had you and that was always enough."

Reaching across the dining table, Zoe lays a hand over her mother's. "You've always been the best. I can talk to you more than any friends I've ever had."

"What a lovely compliment," Carly smiles, her brown eyes misting over.

"It's true," Zoe insists. "You never judge or force your own opinions onto me. I feel very lucky to have you as my mum."

"Yet you've only told me about these letters because one was delivered here," Carly reminds her.

Looking shamefaced, Zoe uses her fork to play with the food on her plate. "They're the reason I moved in with Palmer," she admits. "Not that I don't love him, I do, and I'm very happy to be with him. I just thought I'd be married first," she tails off, feeling foolish.

"Then move back," Carly suggests. "There's nothing stopping you. Moving in with Palmer hasn't made any difference to whoever is sending you these letters, so why not come back home?"

It was tempting, and sucking in her bottom lip Zoe gives the idea some thought.

Then she smiles and nods. "It would make arranging the wedding so much easier," she tells her mother. "We have so much to do and so little time to do it in. I thought we could go shopping for my wedding dress tomorrow," Zoe suggests, and watches her mother's face light up with joy.

"I can't wait," Carly agrees. "When do you think you'll move back home?"

Hmm, that won't be easy. Palmer is bound to think I'm moving out because of the letters. I have to find a way of making him see that it makes sense.

"I'd better go back tonight and explain it to him. He's bound to think it has something to do with the letters," Zoe tells her mother honestly.

"If he's as innocent of these accusations as you say, then he'll understand," Carly tells her gently.

"He will. I know he will." *I really hope he will.*

<u>CHAPTER NINETEEN</u>

"I'm losing you," Palmer tells her, his face a picture of despair. "Little by little, but the result will be the same."

"No. That just isn't true," Zoe pleads. "I love you. I don't care what the letters say."

"Then why move out? Why leave me if it isn't for the letters?"

"I've told you – I want to do this properly, not because some sicko has panicked us into making hasty decisions. And for me, that means getting married first," she tells him earnestly. "I've even arranged to go wedding dress shopping tomorrow with my mother – why would I do that if I were leaving you permanently?"

Letting out a long sigh, Palmer pushes agitated hands back through his hair and grimaces at the thought of watching Zoe move out.

"It just doesn't feel right. I don't want there to be any distance between us, not in any way shape or form!"

Closing the gap to take him at his word, Zoe puts her arms around his neck and pulls him down for a kiss.

Light and playful, the kiss soon deepens. Each trying to convey to the other how deeply they feel.

"Don't leave me, Zoe," he pleads, his lips to her ear, his teeth gently nibbling and grazing her skin.

"Never!" Her head falls back allowing Palmer to take full advantage of her exposed flesh.

His lips travel downwards, tasting, teasing, finding her jumping pulse and making it jump harder and faster.

"I need you." His voice is low and rough with emotion, and they fall onto the nearest settee, not bothering with the bed even though it is in the same large room.

His hands push at her clothing, easing her out of it, as she helps him out of his.

Naked and fully aroused, Palmer is magnificent in the heat of his passion. And his need excites Zoe all the more.

Her man doesn't just want her; he needs her with an urgency bordering on desperation!

When his lips take her breasts she cries out at his hunger, yet tenderness is in every move he makes.

His hands caress, take and arouse, and his mouth follows them down to the apex of her sex.

Tasting her, possessing her in this most intimate way, Palmer lays claim to his woman.

Pulling her hips to the edge of the settee he moves to kneel between her thighs and plunges into the heat of her.

They cry out at the intense pleasure of their joining. Deeper, deeper, faster, harder, it's never quite enough.

Their eyes are locked, telling each other without the need for words just what this act means. 'I'm yours, your mine, ever and always'.

She can't doubt him - doesn't doubt him, not when his eyes are telling her that he loves her, that he needs her in his life and beneath his body, to join with him in this beautiful act of love.

But it hasn't changed her mind. Even after, when they lay still joined and naked in each other's arms, Zoe knows that she needs to move back home.

Silently they move around Palmer's flat, collecting this, packing that, and all the while he feels little pieces of the greater pain he knows will follow when all of Zoe has gone from his home.

They stand together, looking around the vast loft space, checking for anything they may have missed.

"Stay," he implores quietly.

"I can't."

"Then stay just for tonight. I can take you home first thing in the morning."

Shaking her head, tears start to fall down Zoe's cheeks. "It will just make the move even harder," she tells him.

"Not if you really mean to come back," he insists gently.

With a hand to his cheek, Zoe smiles up at him. "I love you, and when we're married I will happily live with you."

Knowing he's fighting a battle that is already lost, Palmer moves in to hold her. "I'll keep you to that, Zoe Benson."

At her mother's house, Zoe uses her key to let them in and helps Palmer with a couple of boxes while he takes the suitcase.

"Hello, Palmer," Carly Benson greets him with a warm smile.

"Just delivering your daughter back, safe and sound," he jokes lamely.

"It's not forever," Carly assures him. And putting a hand to his arm says, "Thank you, Palmer. For giving us this time together before my daughter flies the nest for good."

"When she does, I'll take good care of her," he assures Zoe's mother.

"If I had any doubts about that you can rest assured I would have made them known by now," she smiles more brightly. "As it is, I feel sure that my daughter will be in safe and loving hands."

"If only..." he begins, but thinks better of saying any more.

"The letters?" Carly asks with a raised brow and sees his fly up in surprise. "One was delivered here. Zoe had little choice but to explain, and I'm glad she did; now we can both look out for her."

He nods, but Palmer still isn't easy about this arrangement. "Did she tell you what the letters have been saying about me?"

Nodding, Carly listens to Zoe humming while she puts things away in her bedroom. "Zoe isn't easily influenced," she tells him. "She tends to make up her own mind about things and pretty much sticks to her decisions once they're made."

"So, you're telling me I don't need to worry?"

"If the letters are untrue they can't hurt either of you," Carly states firmly.

If. Such a little word, yet the damage it can wreak with the doubt it implies can be devastating.

When it's time for him to leave, Palmer's heart all but breaks.

"I'll stay over on Sunday, just like we used to," Zoe tells him when they kiss goodbye. "And we'll go into work together on Monday morning, if you still don't mind giving me a lift home after work?"

"Mind? Huh!" he groans. "I'll be wishing every minute were a second until you come back to me. Then I won't want time to move at all!"

"Just remember that I love you," she tells him softly.

Just putting one foot in front of the other to walk down the drive to his car has been difficult, but nothing to the effort Palmer has to put into actually driving away from Zoe's house.

The pain in his chest is almost unbearable, the chasm she has left inside of him feels too deep and wide to survive.

But he will, Palmer determines. Whoever is trying to drive him and Zoe apart will fail spectacularly. And nothing will say that better than their wedding.

Once settled back in his now too enormous loft, Palmer sets about getting the wedding venue set in stone.

If a wedding is what it will take to keep Zoe with him, then he will give her one to enjoy and remember.

Going shopping with her mother is such a joy for Zoe. Moving back home had been the right thing.

"Do you have any idea where you want to look?" her

mother asks while they eat toast and drink tea at the breakfast table next morning.

"No, should we look on the internet for local wedding shops?" Zoe suggests.

Carly nods, "It might help give us some direction, instead of wandering around in the hopes of finding one. Birmingham is too big a place for that!"

"Hmm, I can just imagine my poor feet," Zoe smiles, her excitement shining through.

"Ok, I'll clear while you go on the computer," Carly suggests, and they move to carry out their allotted tasks.

At the first boutique Zoe is told that she needs to make an appointment with a consultant for proper advice and fitting. By the time they reach the third, they have come to realise that this is the norm.

"Ok, one more and then we go home," Zoe moans, all the fun having gone out of her day.

But her luck is in; they aren't completely booked up and only ask that she come back in an hour.

It is almost lunch time by now and so Zoe and her mother go for a coffee and a bite to eat.

"I daren't eat too much if I'm going to be trying on dresses," Zoe laughs, all her enthusiasm back and bubbling over.

While her mother is still at the till paying for their snack, Zoe sends Palmer a text.

I'm so excited, just having coffee then in boutique to try on first dress. Had quick look, all look lovely. I want you to be proud of me on our special day. Zoe xxx

She has just taken the tray from her mother and set out her own cup of coffee and a scone, when her phone pings to let her know she has a message.

"Don't tell me," Carly rolls her eyes but also smiles, "that will be Palmer!"

Snatching up her mobile, Zoe grins when she sees it is indeed her fiancé answering her text.

You will look lovely in whatever you chose to wear. I love you, will always be proud as long as you're mine. Palmer xxx

Feeling a little sad that he still has doubts about her resolve to marry him, Zoe replies; *Always & Forever Yours, Zoe xxx*

Smiling happily to herself, glad that her daughter appears happy and back to her old bubbly self, Carly pours a cup of tea and enjoys a cheese and ham sandwich.

"Are you sure that is going to be enough?" she asks Zoe, looking dubiously at the small scone and jam. "You haven't eaten since breakfast, and even then you only had a round of toast."

"If I have any more I'll look like a blob when I try the dresses on," Zoe states, but smiles brightly enjoying her special mother and daughter day.

"Have you heard from Craig recently?" she asks her mother, and is amazed to see a faint blush tinge her cheeks.

"We've been in touch," Carly tells her daughter cagily.

"And...?" Zoe prompts impatiently.

"And we may go out for a meal together next Saturday, if the hotel work goes as expected," she smiles over at Zoe.

"Good! I'm really pleased that you're seeing someone," Zoe grins, genuinely pleased for her mum. "You deserve to find someone special."

"Well, let's not jump the gun – it's only a meal," Carly laughs, some of Zoe's excitement rubbing off on her.

"It's just the beginning, you see!"

Trying on wedding dresses is not only exciting, it is emotional. Especially for the mother of the bride whose eyes well up with every dress her daughter tries on.

"Oh, Zoe, you look so lovely," Carly expounds, as she has for the other three dresses that Zoe has tried on.

"You said that before," Zoe giggles. "How am I supposed to know which is the best one if you love them all?"

Going back into the curtained off changing area, Zoe tries on the dress she initially picked out. She isn't sure that this dress will suit her shorter stature, even in the 4 inch heels she brought with her.

But she couldn't have been more wrong. This time when her mother sees her, the tears can't be held back.

The dress is by Veni Infantino, and Zoe is stunned to see herself wearing it.

Walking towards the full-length wall of mirrors, she sees an elegant young woman with large, round eyes looking back at her.

The dress is cut in simple lines, and has a lace, three-quarter sleeve shrug type high necked jacket to go with it. The semi-fitted body gently flares from the hip to swirl at the feet and has a matching top layer of fine lace.

Turning to Carly, she simply says, "Mum...?"

"I've never seen you look more beautiful! You look..." But words fail her and the assistant passes her a handy box of tissues.

"You'll need to come back for a proper fitting," the bridal consultant tells Zoe. "And you'll need to be wearing the same underwear and shoes that you'll be wearing on your big day."

Looking wide eyed, Zoe turns to her mum. "But we haven't bought them yet!"

"Then you'd best buy them today," the young woman tells her. "Usually we take orders 6 months prior to the wedding to enable us to guarantee supply of the gown on time. Let me just see when I can book you in for a first fitting."

Taking the opportunity to walk back and forth, Zoe loves the feel of the beautiful gown. But then she frowns, her brown eyes clouding over with concern.

"Mum, I know you said you wanted to pay for my wedding dress, but we didn't actually check how much this dress it?"

Shaking her head while still wiping at her eyes, Carly looks lovingly on her grown up daughter.

"I don't care if I have to take out a mortgage, you're having that dress – it's so lovely on you. It's perfect!"

Zoe grins with delight, "It is, isn't it! I think Palmer will agree, too."

A couple of hours later, with wedding shoes and underwear bought and paid for, the two women head home.

"What about bridesmaids, are you having any?" Carly asks as she pours herself and Zoe a welcome cup of tea.

Frowning, Zoe sips at her tea and thinks about it. She doesn't really have any close female friends; perhaps she could just have Laura as a maid of honour.

"I'm not really sure about that. I've lost touch with a lot of my old college friends and I'm not sure if Laura will want to be a maid of honour on her own?"

"Well you've got plenty of time to think about it. Maybe you'd want one or two of your cousins as bridesmaids. Stella's twins would make the ideal pageboy and flower girl," Carly suggests helpfully.

"That's a great idea. Let's give aunt Rose a call tonight!"

I'm so, so lucky! I have a wonderful man who loves me and a family that I can rely on. I don't think I've ever felt more loved and cared for.

CHAPTER TWENTY

Connor looks tanned and fit when Zoe meets up with him at his and Palmer's mother's house for dinner.

"Did you miss me?" he asks her as he passes Zoe a glass of white wine.

"How was Sorrento?" she asks instead of answering him. "You look like you made time for some sunbathing."

"You have got to be kidding!" he scoffs. "Craig is a tough work-master – no doubt on my big brother's orders. So no, I didn't get to sunbathe, but I did work outside with my shirt off. The local girls loved it," he grins suggestively.

"And where is Laura tonight?" Palmer asks, having overheard Connor's last comment.

"Laura isn't my keeper! I'll see her when I get around to it and in my own good time!"

"She's a good woman, Connor, don't hurt her," Palmer warns him.

Narrowing his eyes, Connor isn't sure to what Palmer is referring. "If you're so damned fond of her, you go out with her," he offers sarcastically.

"I've already got a good woman, I don't need anyone else!" Palmer smiles over at Zoe and gets a shy smile in reply.

"That's not what I heard," Connor sneers bitterly. "I heard she packed up and went running home to mummy!"

Dorothy becomes aware of the tension between her sons when she turns to speak to Zoe. Frowning at them both, she doesn't need words to bring them into line.

"I hear you went wedding shopping with your mother, Zoe. Did you find anything nice?" Dorothy asks too brightly.

"As a matter of fact..." and she turns to smile at Palmer to include him in the conversation, "...I bought a wedding dress! Or at least, my mum bought it for me – she insisted," Zoe adds when Palmer's smile slips.

"Oh, my dear, how exciting! I wish I could have been there – with no daughters I'll never get that privilege," she laments.

"I'm so sorry, I didn't think," Zoe exclaims sadly.

"Not to worry, it really is a mother and daughter experience," Dorothy concedes with good grace. "But I'd like to hear a few details after dinner," she grins impishly. "Once the men are out of earshot, of course!"

Despite her best efforts to ignore him, Zoe can't help noticing Connor's brooding stares in her direction.

Why didn't he bring Laura with him tonight? He doesn't seem very happy with his own company, and I wish he'd stop staring at me like he's got something to say! Damn it, I usually like coming to Dorothy's for dinner once a week, but maybe I'll have to reconsider if he's going to behave like a spoiled brat!

"I'm sorry," Zoe looks up at Palmer, realising that he is talking to her. "What was that?"

"I said, we won another big contract today," Palmer repeats, smiling at her indulgently. "There was some stiff competition for it, too."

Beaming with pride, Zoe reaches across the table and takes his hand. "That's wonderful news. When does it start?"

"Is this the new community centre you were telling me about?" his father asks, and the conversation for the rest of the meal revolves around Palmer's good news.

The only person not taking part in that conversation is Connor. He looks more sullen than ever, even more irked by his 'golden boy' big brother's business success, and the pride his parents show in it.

I'm sick to death of this family revolving around Mr Fucking Do Right! Can't anyone talk about anything else? Has anyone even bothered to ask about the job in Italy? You'd think I was invisible for all the notice anyone takes of my being home, if they even noticed that I was gone in the first damned place!

The more praise Palmer gets, the more Connor broods. It has always been the same, even when they were kids.

Palmer this and Palmer that, and Connor stop this and Connor stop that. It seems like Palmer can do no wrong while Connor can do nothing right!

And I tried, didn't I? I studied at school, just not as nerdily as my brother. And I achieved a few good grades, just not the A's and B's that Palmer did.

But his parents had taken Palmer's side on everything. And even when it came to presents, Palmer always got the best. But Connor had seen to it that he hadn't kept them long.

Too fucking right! If I want something I take it, and as Palmer always gets the best I usually take it from him!

He stares at Zoe, wondering what a girl like that really sees in his boring brother. Surely she'd enjoy a little fun;

he could give her a good time if he had his brother's money.

That's probably all she stays with him for. But I'll soon put that right!

When they all move into the conservatory, Connor makes his excuses and his escape.

Zoe is relieved when Connor leaves, and begins to relax and enjoy the evening.

What no one realises is that Connor has big plans. All of which involve his brother, some of which involve Zoe, and all of which will see him coming off the better man!

The next few weeks pass quickly. Zoe is busy at work and at home. Palmer's business is booming; more men have been taken on and she has had to interview more office staff to cope with the increased workload there too.

But the wedding is what is consuming every hour outside of work. Along with her mother, Zoe is planning it all. Palmer has long since insisted on picking up the entire bill, even offering to reimburse Carly for the cost of her daughter's wedding gown – but on that she had been firm.

Zoe is proud of her mother for sticking to her guns – it had been really nice of Palmer to offer to cover the cost, but it is something that Carly wants to do for her daughter by herself.

Her father may have walked out on her early in her life, but Zoe's mother has never left her wanting for any essentials.

She hadn't always been able to go on every school trip – some of them had cost a small fortune, but Zoe had always understood that her mother gave her what she could.

They had always been a good team, and now they are a great team, organising a wedding in double quick time.

"Did you send the approved Order of Service design back to the printers?" Carly asks while trawling through the wedding list that Zoe has drawn up with Palmer.

"I did, they will be so lovely," Zoe enthuses. "And the Psalm readings we chose are beautiful – you're still ok with doing that, aren't you?"

Carly has volunteered to read the Psalms that Zoe and Palmer have chosen, and Dorothy is to read a poem that she and Bill had found and shown them.

"The hymns are lovely too," Carly adds wistfully. "I always have loved 'Bind us Together Lord', it's one of my favourites."

"And with the words printed in the Order of Service, it will make it easier for everyone, instead of having to find it in a separate hymn book," Zoe observes with satisfaction. "Have you ticked off all the replies we've got so far?"

Nodding, Carly looks down the wedding list and then over at her daughter. "So far you haven't received any refusals. If it carries on like this the wedding will be enormous!"

"Hmm, it can't be helped. Palmer has a lot of relations. He has aunts and uncles on both sides and they have a fair few children too."

"Good job you're not overrun with family or this wedding would be ridiculous!"

"The manor house that Palmer found is stunning, and it has a hall that will fit everyone in comfortably. Even if all of the invited guests turn up," Zoe laughs. She really is enjoying herself and is looking forward to her big day.

She looks across at her mother, busily organising piles of paper, putting order into the chaos.

"Thanks mum. Thanks for my beautiful wedding gown and for all your help with all of this," Zoe tells her, sweeping a hand over the piles of lists and printouts that surround them on the living-room floor.

"Are you kidding? I'm in my element," Carly laughs. "This is every mother's dream. I'm just so happy for you, darling. Palmer is such a good man, and it's obvious that he loves you very much."

Frowning, Zoe thinks about her mother and father's wedding day.

"You must have thought that about dad once," she observes quietly. "I'm really sorry that he hurt you like that."

For a moment, Carly is thrown back into the past, to the excitement of arranging her own wedding. Douglas Benson had been so handsome; an up and coming actor he was charming and fascinating.

And she had fallen hard and fast for the talented thespian. He'd courted her, pursued her to the point where she hadn't been able to turn around without finding a bouquet of flowers or an invitation to go to dinner or the opera, or some other glamorous place with him. And in the end he had begged her to marry him, had told her that she was his heart's desire and he couldn't live without her.

But he had lived without her. Just three years after their large white wedding, her world had been torn asunder.

It was during the shooting of his second big film that he'd fallen deeply in love with his young leading lady. So much so that he'd pleaded with his wife and mother of his baby daughter, to release him from their wedding vows and grant him a divorce.

He had broken her heart and destroyed her self-esteem into the bargain. But she had determined not to let his selfishness drag her and her daughter down. She would be a good breadwinner, would meet her daughter's needs without resorting to begging her ex-husband for anything.

"Life goes on," is all Carly tells her daughter. "After a time of mourning the loss, life just has to go on. And I had you," she smiles more brightly. "He gave me everything when he gave me you. Don't ever think that I regret the life I've had with you."

Kneeling up, Zoe wraps her arms around her mother's neck and says, "I love you, mum. You're the best!"

<u>CHAPTER TWENTY-ONE</u>

In Miami, Florida, there is a discussion going on about backdrops, locations and co-stars.

Douglas Benson is being taken through the details of his next film.

"And how long will I need to be on location?" he asks, growing tired of discussing business in the heat of the day.

Not that he's really interested. He hasn't been able to concentrate on anything properly since reading the newspaper article his assistant had brought to his notice.

It was about a young businessman, a good-news story telling of his success in building his own construction firm from next to nothing and most intriguingly, had told of his up-coming marriage to Miss Zoe Benson, his 20 year old fiancée.

Twenty! Has it really been 20 years since I last saw

Carly? She was a looker back then; I wonder what she looks like now. Probably put on a few pounds, but then who hasn't? And Zoe; my daughter is 20 now. A bit young for getting married! Still, Carly had only just turned 20 when we got married and we were happy enough.

Till we weren't. I was an idiot. That bimbo I married after Carly wasn't a patch on her. I didn't realise what I had until it was gone – a well worn phrase, but true never-the-less!

"Are you even listening?" his producer asks Douglas irritably.

"Yes. Yes. Just cut to the chase man!" Douglas smiles dully.

But Douglas isn't listening; his thoughts are off in the past thinking about a daughter he wants more and more to see.

When Zoe gets into work, she goes straight to Laura's office to speak to her.

"Hey, how are you doing?" she greets her friend.

"Hi, ok, you?" Laura grins happily.

"Tired, my mum and I are up late most nights going over wedding plans. Did you go for your fitting this weekend?"

Laura had agreed to be her maid-of-honour, and accompanying her would be a tiny flower girl and pageboy.

"I did, and it really is perfect," Laura enthuses. "I met up with your cousin, Stella, and her twins. You should have seen how cute Jake looked in his pageboy outfit, and Jessie was absolutely gorgeous in her dress and holding the little basket. They are both so adorable."

"I did see them," Zoe laughs. "Stella took photos and sent them to me. She was thrilled when I asked if they could take part in my wedding."

"Well, of course she was," Laura tells her. "Most mums love the chance to show off their little darlings. And they really are little darlings. I don't remember ever meeting two such well behaved 3 year olds."

"Good to hear. Let's hope they behave as nicely on the big day," Zoe frowns, then smiles contentedly. "I did have second and third thoughts about them being so young, but hey, it's a family wedding and kids misbehave all the time, right?"

"Dead right!" Laura agrees, and both girls laugh at their too serious conversation.

"By the way, I ran into Connor last night. Are you two still seeing each other?"

Laura hesitates in answering. "I think so, but Connor hasn't been over yet since he's been back from Italy."

Feeling awkward, Zoe tries to smooth things over. "He said Craig has been working them like slaves for weeks.

He's probably catching up on some much needed sleep. I bet he'll be in touch in the next few days."

"Hmm," Laura murmurs. "Or maybe he's bored with me and wants to move on?"

Wanting to tell her friend that it would be no loss if he did, it takes Zoe a lot of effort to say, "Don't be daft. He wouldn't find anyone better than you and he knows it."

"I'm not so sure. Sometimes I wonder if he even likes me, let alone loves me," Laura says tellingly.

"Then you should look for someone who can appreciate what a lovely person you are," Zoe exclaims, her dislike of Connor finally getting the better of her.

Changing the uncomfortable subject, Laura asks, "Have you had any more of those awful letters? You haven't mentioned them in a while?"

Heaving a large sigh, Zoe shakes her head. "The last one was over a month ago, nearer two, but it was nasty and took a bit of getting over."

"I can't help but ask, what did it say?" Laura grimaces, unable to stem her curiosity.

"It actually accused Palmer of being the father of a child that he doesn't care about. But he denies everything and says he can't imagine why anyone would make up such obvious lies. But I could tell it hurt him," Zoe says, her brown eyes clouding over as she remembers Palmer's reaction.

"And you're still no nearer to finding out whose sending them?"

"No. And it really scared me when it turned up at my mum's house." Zoe shudders, remembering how vulnerable she'd felt. "It was like I was being stalked. But the one good thing to come out of it was me moving back home. It's been great having time with my mum, planning the wedding together and looking forward to the big day."

"Just eight weeks to go, oooohhhh," Laura's eyes go dramatically wide and both girls let out an excited scream.

"So this is what you get up to when the boss is late in," Palmer says, putting on a stern face as he regards the two young women.

Turning, Zoe smiles up at him and just laughs. "Be right with you, Sir, just talking to my maid of honour about my wedding plans."

"Oh, well, that's alright then," Palmer grins, and pulls Zoe in for a kiss.

"Sir!" she admonishes him playfully. "Not in front of other people - whatever will they think?!"

Laura giggles, enjoying their little act, but secretly envying them too.

If only Connor were more like you. At least Zoe knows you love her.

Palmer is in his office for the rest of the day. Zoe gets

on with her work and the hours pass quickly.

"Are you coming back to mine tonight?" Palmer asks when Zoe brings him in a mug of black coffee.

"Yes, I already told mum not to expect me home for dinner so we can go straight from work," she smiles, sliding her bottom onto the edge of his desk in front of Palmer. "Of course, that does mean you'll have to feed me," and she grins at him with a raised brow.

"My pleasure. What would madam like – Chinese or Indian takeaway, or would madam like to go out for dinner?"

Zoe laughs at Palmer's exaggerated English gentleman's accent. "You idiot! How about we get some shopping on the way home and I'll cook?"

Pulling her into his lap, Palmer kisses her soundly. "Sounds great – then I get you all to myself and we can have sex for afters!"

"Palmer! The door isn't properly closed – what if someone hears you?"

"So what if they do. They'll go home tonight full of envy," he chuckles softly, his voice a sexy moan close to her ears.

Zoe squirms in his lap and has Palmer moaning louder, hardening uncomfortably beneath her weight.

"Zoe..." His lips find her ear and now she is moaning,

trying not to give in to the sensations he's causing her aroused young body to feel.

Palmer's hand slips between them, cupping her and easing her panties aside. He's pleased to find her as aroused as he is and slips a finger inside her moist heat.

Undoing his fly, he eases his erection out and turns her on his lap so that one leg is either side of him, then lowers her until he fills her.

"Oh my god, Palmer!"

But her protest isn't long lived. Holding her hips he moves her, pushing into her until her groans grow louder.

To quiet them, Palmer closes his mouth over hers and swallows the sounds, until suddenly her head falls back.

Her climax is hard and fast and her cries are loud. Palmer follows her over the edge all too soon and has to stifle his own vocal response.

With her forehead on his shoulder, Zoe tries to catch her breath.

"I do not believe we just did that!"

"We're not safe yet," Palmer reminds her, pulling tissues from a drawer and aiding Zoe to right herself.

"That was...bloody amazing," Palmer laughs when his own clothing is straightened and he looks up into Zoe's shocked face.

"You are a pervert," she accuses, but smiles as she draws in her bottom lip.

"And you are the sweetest prude I've ever had the pleasure of having sex with," he laughs, watching her blush deepen.

"Well, that's the first and last time that will happen," Zoe tells him sternly. "What if someone had come in, I'd never have been able to show my face in the office again!"

"Spoil-sport," he teases, but determines to keep himself under better control in future.

On the way home they pick up steaks and veg with a few potatoes and mushrooms. Then call into an off-license to pick up a couple of bottles of wine.

"I meant to put an order in, but keep forgetting," Palmer tells her as he pulls out of the parking space. "I usually stock up on wine every couple of months, and they do some good deals if you order enough in one go."

Smiling, Zoe has to remind herself that Palmer is actually a millionaire. He has no airs and graces, no pretence about him whatsoever. And he still shops at the local supermarket and off-licence!

As they eat their meal, Zoe fills Palmer in on her mother's and Craig Stanley's little assignation.

"She told me that Craig was a complete gentleman," Zoe states happily. "And they're planning on seeing each other again!"

"So, you think there's a romance in the offing?" Palmer leans in, encouraging Zoe's conjecture.

"I do! And I'm very pleased about it," she states boldly. "He sounds nice, and you can vouch for him, right?"

Palmer sits back in his seat, obviously considering her question. Rubbing his chin, Palmer pulls his brows into a comical frown, "Well, I don't know. I've never known Craig go jelly-kneed over a woman before! He's been out with a few, was actually engaged once, but since Abbey died I haven't seen him look at a woman the way he looks at your mother."

"Abbie? Whose Abbie, and when did she die?" Zoe asks, worried now.

"Abbie was Craig's fiancée – he loved her more than life," Palmer states softly. "If he could have donated something to ward off the cancer, he would have given her anything. It brought the big man to his knees when she passed away."

Tears spring into Zoe's eyes, and her bottom lip is now tucked between her teeth to stop it quivering.

"That's so sad. And he never found anyone else?"

Shaking his head, Palmer takes her hand. "For some men, men like me and Craig, there's only one love of your life, the rest are just second best."

Blinking in surprise, Zoe pulls her hand back. "I don't think I want my mother to be second best even to a dead woman," she tells him, then blanches at her own words. "I mean, I feel for her, and for Craig, but my mother deserves to be loved wholeheartedly for the kind woman that she is."

"And I'm sure Craig would agree with you," Palmer tries to extricate his size 10's from his mouth. "I just meant, the big man won't settle for just any woman. She'll have to be very special to catch Craig – as I'm sure your mother is," he adds quickly.

CHAPTER TWENTY-TWO

Having turned down the starring role in a major film, Douglas Benson is waiting in an airport lounge for his flight to Birmingham, England.

He'd thought about it long and hard, had changed his mind a hundred and one times, then he'd made his reservation and packed his suitcases.

He is going to England to meet his daughter. And if he manages to catch up with Carly at the same time, that would be all to the good.

Douglas has often fantasised about going back. *What will Carly do, will she welcome me with open arms, or has she turned into a shrew who will shout and scream at me for having left her?*

He shudders at that last thought. But life isn't like the movies – he knows that from his own experiences.

Having married three times since leaving Carly, he's never found the kind of love he once shared with her.

His flight is called and Douglas finds himself eager to board the plane. He's never liked flying, but Carly and Zoe are in England so that is where he wants to be.

The wedding planner for the Heathley Manor House takes Palmer and Zoe on a tour of the venue to give them an outline of their wedding day.

They have decided to use one of the halls for the main service; decked with flowers and satin sashes, a small raised stage with a decorative lectern standing on it will serve for the readings.

"It will be beautiful," the woman assures them. "An aisle will be formed down the centre of rows of seats, along which a red carpet will be laid. At either side of the carpet small sculptured stands will be dotted at intervals and swags of flowers will hang like a rope from one to another.

Three stanchions of flowers will decorate either side of the raised front stage, going from tallest to moderate to smaller, giving the effect of framing the area." The woman is precise and gives the impression that nothing can possibly go wrong.

"Special white chairs will be placed for the bride and groom to use while the readings are given and hymns are sung – unless you wish to remain standing, of course."

Neither Palmer nor Zoe contradict the woman's plans, they sound perfect.

"And once the service has been completed, you will move to one side, to a table here," and she waves a hand off to the right, "where you will sign your wedding licence, along with your selected witnesses. Time will, of course, be given to take photographs as you wish, and for family and friends to do the same.

If you'll follow me," she smiles and leads the way out of a set of double doors and into an even larger hall, "this will be your reception room. As you have requested a sit down meal, this will be served by our staff along with wine, and water will be placed on each table.

The Champagne toast will be brought out by our wait staff, already poured and distributed to your top table and to your guests. Over here, to the right of the top table, will be the wedding cake, properly displayed according to the design you choose. Again photographs will, of course, be facilitated, and once you indicate that you are ready for us to do so, the cake will be taken and cut into portions for your guests to share in.

Any questions so far?" she asks, taking a breather from her monologue.

"It all sounds rather splendid," Zoe says, feeling a little

in awe of the woman and the grand plans she has for their wedding day.

But Palmer is frowning. "What about the wedding photos – when do we get the chance to have those taken?"

Zoe thinks he's found a chink in the woman's plans, but she just smiles and nods.

"I've saved the best till last. Please, come with me," and she walks them back into the room where the wedding service will be and out through another set of double doors to a garden that takes their breath away.

"Oh, Palmer, this is wonderful. It's absolutely perfect," Zoe cries, a hand flying up to cover her mouth as tears form in her amazed eyes.

"You really like it?" he asks, pleased that she seems to be happy with his choice of venue.

"Like is not the word for how I feel – I'm so very lucky. No bride ever had a wedding such as ours will be." And she flings her arms about his neck and bursts into tears.

"In case of rain," the woman begins again when Zoe pulls herself together with the help of a handkerchief from Palmer, "there is an arched area that is fully undercover but which looks out over the hills and rear gardens. You will not be disappointed, whatever the weather," she assures them kindly.

Looking around her, smiling at the impressive grounds, Zoe looks back at the manor house and frowns.

"What's wrong?" Palmer asks, ever on the alert.

"It's just...well, this is beautiful, and it would make the perfect venue..."

"But..." Palmer urges Zoe to speak her mind.

"But it's so far out – how will our guests travel here," she asks. "And, forgive me for saying but, I can't imagine all of them would be able to afford the price of an overnight stay after the wedding either."

Shocked as Palmer begins to laugh and the wedding planner smiles knowingly, Zoe's frown only deepens.

"It's all taken care of," he smiles. "I've taken all the rooms here and at the nearby Malty Hotel for two nights. The night before and the night of the wedding," he states with satisfaction.

"You...you did!"

"I did. And a small fleet of transport has been laid on to ferry guests from the Malty to here for the wedding and back again at the end of the night."

"You've really thought of everything," Zoe gasps as she realises the full extent to which Palmer has gone to give them a very special wedding day.

With a hand to her cheek, Palmer gazes down into pools of melted brown chocolate and sees all the love he feels for Zoe reflected right back at him.

"I want to marry you more than I want to take my next breath. I love you, Zoe Benson, soon to be Mrs Zoe Johnson."

"And I love you, Palmer Johnson, soon to be husband of Mrs Zoe Johnson."

It has taken a small miracle but the wedding plans are all complete.

Money, of course, can make small miracles that much easier to perform. And Zoe doesn't doubt that Palmer has greased the wheels to make the event happen just when and how they want it to happen.

But she can't find it in her to be unhappy about it. Yes it feels decadent, but it's a once in a lifetime commitment and why shouldn't they enjoy the fruits of Palmer's hard labour.

Then Zoe has a thought that strikes at her heart. *I don't have anyone to give me away! How could I have overlooked that!*

Walking out of Birmingham Airport, Douglas Benson looks tanned and handsome as he gazes about him.

I need a hire car, but a taxi will do for now. I wonder if Carly is still living in the same area. I bet she is, she hates change and loves to wallow in the familiar.

Right then; better make my way to Fowlmere Road and do some asking about.

When the taxi pulls up outside of his old house, Douglas is swamped by memories and love.

He'd lived here before hitting it big, with his wife and their little baby daughter.

It had been a home filled with love, until he'd gone and ruined it all. *Why!* He'd often asked himself that. *Why couldn't it have been enough?*

He watches someone walking around the lounge, then sees her stand at the bay window as if looking out for someone.

No! It can't be! Douglas has to stop himself from climbing out of the taxi and running up to the house to see Carly. For there she stands, in the same house where she had been his wife.

Then a large man comes to stand behind her, too close to be just an acquaintance.

What did you expect, you idiot! That she'd be pining for you to come back. That she would have waited all alone for all these years just on the off-chance that you might change your mind and come back to her!

Well he has. But the lady is obviously no longer available.

He asks the taxi driver to take him to a Holiday Inn he knows of, off the M6 and books himself in. The odd person or two gives him a second glance like, 'don't I know you from somewhere'. But Douglas has always found that when he returns to England, which he has done often over the years, if you act like everyone else around you then no one really takes any notice. Not too much anyway.

Though it's often different in The States. There the average Joe is more 'star' savvy, always on the lookout for the 'famous' shopper, or face in the crowd to have their photo taken with.

Whilst he unpacks, Douglas thinks about his daughter.

I wonder if Zoe still lives there too. Or maybe she's moved out on her own, or in with a friend to share the rent.

Christ, I should have kept in contact. But a clean break seemed to be the best thing at the time. Now I'll be lucky if she gives me the time of day, let alone an invitation to her wedding.

Married! My little girl is getting married. And I only know about it because her future husband had an article written about him that my assistant found.

Pure chance. It has to mean something when fate steps in to bring us all back together. Maybe he's just a friend, he tells himself, his thoughts flicking back to Carly, *or someone she's just met who hasn't gotten his feet under the table yet. Yeah, that's it!*

Getting showered and changed, Douglas is feeling a bit jet-lagged and decides to take a nap before paying a visit to his ex-wife.

I don't want her to see me looking tired and worn out. Not the impression I want to make at all!

The minute Zoe and Palmer returned to his loft flat, they had made long, slow, passionate love.

Still lying together, they're legs entwined and their smiles content, Zoe voices her concern.

"Palmer, I don't know how I haven't thought of it before but, I don't have anyone to give me away at the wedding," she states softly.

"What? Christ, what an idiot!" Then he laughs at her incredulous face. "Not you, sweetheart, I meant me. It never even crossed my mind!"

"It doesn't seem to have occurred to anyone, even my mother," Zoe exclaims, her voice rising in panic.

"Ok. Ok. Let's think about this coolly and logically," Palmer suggests. "My dad would love to do it, and he already has his suit being made."

But Zoe's worried eyes look down at her tangled fingers. "It should be someone from my side of the family. But the only person I can think of is not someone you would want to stand up and make a speech. My uncle Mike can be a bit unpredictable and his sense of humour more than a bit risqué, if you see what I mean?"

"Ah, well, probably not a good idea then. But we'll think of something," he assures her. "Perhaps we should speak to your mother, she may have the perfect 'uncle' hiding in the family closet somewhere," he laughs softly, trying to lift her mood.

"Ok. Maybe." I really hope so!

<u>CHAPTER TWENTY-THREE</u>

When Zoe and Palmer arrive at her mother's house, a strange car is parked out front blocking the drive.

"A bit cheeky," Zoe comments as she and Palmer make their way past it up to the house.

Turning her key in the lock, Zoe makes to call out to her mother but hears raised voices coming from the lounge.

Looking back at Palmer, she is worried by the strange voice and allows him to enter the lounge ahead of her.

"For heaven's sake, Carly, I just want to see my daughter. Is that really too much to ask?" Douglas Benson insists, keeping his voice on as even a keel as he can in the circumstances. He knows losing his temper with Carly won't get him anywhere. She's a stubborn woman, that hasn't changed in 20 years!

Carly's eyes swing to the opening lounge door and open wide with shock when Palmer and then Zoe walk into the room.

Silence! It is heavy and palpable.

Douglas and Zoe stand eyeing each other, him with hope in his eyes, her with a mixture of curiosity and shock in hers.

"You are my dad? My real dad?"

He nods, not able to speak past the lump in his throat.

You're beautiful. Absolutely beautiful. And I'm a damned fool!

"I'm sorry, Zoe," her mother begins, "I tried to make him leave. I didn't want him to upset you before the wedding. I can't think why you had to come here," she tells Douglas, turning furious eyes back to him. "It will only bring heartache and pain. Didn't you leave us with enough of that the last time you were here?!"

Feeling like a complete heel, Douglas nods forlornly. That wasn't his intent, but it seems that time doesn't heal all ills.

"I'll go, I didn't come here to cause trouble or upset," he tells no one in particular, and picks up his rental car keys to go.

"No, wait!" Zoe cries out, before she has even thought about it. "I mean, can't we at least talk. Isn't that what you came here for?"

Lifting his eyes to Carly, Douglas asks the silent question. *Stay or go, it's up to you now.*

Carly tuts then shrugs. "It's up to you, but I don't want any part in this," and she picks up her handbag and leaves the room.

"I'm sorry," Douglas begins, then lifts his hands palms up in the air and lets them fall hopelessly to his side.

"Why are you here?" Zoe asks abruptly, her forthright manner taking her father by surprise.

"Actually, it was your fiancé here, who brought me back," he tells her, and Zoe looks up at Palmer in surprise.

"I don't know anything about it," Palmer states quickly, holding his hands up to declare his innocence.

"No. No. It was an article that my assistant found. It was about a young local man made good – you," he nods towards Palmer. "It told about how you'd built your business up from nothing into a large and growing empire. And it also mentioned that you were getting married, and to whom."

"Ah," Palmer murmurs. "That was a while ago. I'd forgotten about that."

"Good grief; and your assistant found that all the way over in America?"

It was a telling question and Douglas didn't miss the implications of it.

"How do you know that I live in America?" he asks in a low quiet voice.

Zoe can't hide the heat in her cheeks as two pairs of eyes stare at her.

"Well, mum told me you were an actor; that you went off with your leading lady," she adds, trying to turn some of the attention away from herself. But when it doesn't work she continues, "I just followed the celebrity gossip."

"So, you know more about me than I do about you," Douglas guesses. "Still, if you'll let me, I'd like to put that right."

"Why?" she asks simply, wondering why he has suddenly turned up out of the blue.

"I...I always wanted to keep in touch..." he hesitates, not sure how honest to be, then decides it has to be all or nothing. "I realised shortly after marrying Zara, that I'd made a huge mistake. Not just in marrying her, but in leaving your mother and you," he frowns, trying to find the words to explain properly.

"This world I live in, it isn't real. None of it," he emphasises. "You get carried along by the emotions of the day, sometimes you act on them and sometimes they are fleeting enough to have gone before you can.

"You and your mother were the only real, solid part of my life and I was stupid enough to let you go – and then there was no turning back," he admits quietly.

"So, you allowed your pride to stop you from trying," Zoe guesses, and knows she hit a bull's-eye when his cheeks pink up. "Well, I'd like to say I'd have done things differently, but I'm not sure I would have in your circumstances. We all make mistakes; just don't expect to walk back into our lives like it didn't matter that you left — because it did. It does!"

It is as much as Douglas has a right to expect. *But what about Carly, will she allow me back into her life? And what about the man I saw her with through the window — does she love him, is he living here?*

"Just give me a chance to know you, that's all I ask," Douglas pleads. "I know I don't have the right to ask even that, but if you can see your way to allowing me back into your life, I promise you, I will never let you down again!"

Now that she has gotten over the shock, Zoe actually starts to feel the emotions behind it.

Tears build in her eyes and her bottom lip begins to quiver, "You get one chance, if you blow it I won't look back when I walk away from you."

"Agreed," Douglas nods and takes a step forward, but doesn't close the gap.

She realises that he is leaving that up to her, and Zoe only hesitates for a moment.

He is so solid, so real, that his arms about her can in no way be a childish dream.

For so long she has wanted her father to be in her life, and now, right before her wedding, here he is.

"I suppose an invite to the wedding might be pushing my luck?" he asks, drying her tears with a handkerchief from his pocket.

Zoe looks at Palmer and gets the nod along with a happy smile.

"Actually, there's a starring role up for grabs, if you think you're up to it," she tells him, then finds herself biting down hard on her bottom lip nervously.

"You mean...you would actually allow me..." Now it is Douglas's turn to swallow back tears. He is so overcome that Zoe has to give him back his handkerchief.

"Only if you mean it, about being a part of my life from now on," Zoe murmurs.

And he nods, blows his nose noisily, and nods again. "I can only think you get your compassion from your mother – Carly always did have a big heart."

"Problem solved," Palmer grins at the two of them. "Now our day will be perfect!"

"How about I take you two out for dinner this evening?" Douglas offers brightly. "I'd ask your mother too, but I don't think she would accept."

"Actually, Carly has been seeing a bit of a friend of mine," Palmer tells him, deciding to clear the air. "So don't take it personally, or not all of it anyway."

"Ah. Right. I see," Douglas nods sadly. "But what about you two, will you allow me this small indulgence? We could discuss the wedding, the suit I'll need to get made quick smart?"

Putting a hand to her forehead, Zoe has to take a deep breath to steady her. "I just can't believe how much has happened in one day. One minute we're looking around the most beautiful venue, and then I realise that I don't have anyone to walk me down the aisle...and now, here you are," she says, wafting a hand in her father's direction. "You couldn't write fiction any stranger than that!"

"Fate," Douglas states easily. "I'm a great believer in fate!"

They meet up later that evening at the Holiday Inn off the M6, where Douglas is staying.

"You found it alright then," he greets them cheerfully in the hotel's reception.

The restaurant is superb and the service exemplary. Zoe has an idea that someone has sussed her father's identity.

"We seem to be getting the star treatment," she

whispers over to her father. "Do you think someone recognised you?"

"I don't know, but I'm not complaining. This has been one of the best meals I've had in a long while," he laughs happily. "But then, maybe the company has had something to do with that."

Zoe grins; the evening has gone much easier than she could have hoped for. "Shall we take our drinks through to the lounge? We can relax and talk weddings."

Her father laughs again, enjoying her girlish excitement. "I've missed out on so much. I wish I'd seen you as a girl, I'll bet you loved Christmas — and I would have loved spoiling you."

Father and daughter look at each other with a feeling of loss.

"I'm sorry, Zoe, I was a foolish young man with more ego than heart. But if it's any consolation, I soon regretted my actions and have done so ever since."

"But you mean to make up for it now," she smiles. "As long as you don't walk away, I won't either," she promises, and puts her arm through his and walks into the lounge with Palmer bringing up the rear.

CHAPTER TWENTY-FOUR

The Heathley Manor House is a hive of activity. Downstairs the staff are placing rows of chairs ready for the 2 o'clock wedding service. Flowers are being arranged and the red carpet laid.

In the reception room, tables are being set with finest linen, cutlery polished to sparkle and set out precisely.

A seating order is being followed and place name cards set out accordingly.

The top table, that will seat the bride and groom and their immediate wedding party, is especially beautiful.

Swags of flowers are draped all along the sides and front of the long table, with a pair of crystal swans with their necks intertwined lovingly set in front of the bride and groom.

Over 200 guests will be in attendance and a multitude of wait staff will be on hand to see to their every need.

The day has started early and bright and the bride and her party are already up.

The grooms party are staying in the same building, but are housed in a separate wing so that the bride and groom will have no chance of a premature meeting. Something thought to be bad luck in many circles.

In the brides quarters, the hair, make-up and manicurists are already busy looking after the female family members.

Even Jessie and Jake, the 3 year old twins, are having a great time.

"Here, Jessie, sit on Moma's knee so that the nice lady can do your hair," Zoe's aunt Rose tells her granddaughter, who thankfully obeys. "Jake, don't go off, it'll be your turn next," she warns Jessie's twin brother.

The atmosphere is positively bubbling; chatter is happy and loud, giggles are shared and poor Laura suffers a bout of the hiccups.

"What will I do if it doesn't stop?" she asks. "I can't walk down the aisle yelping like a puppy dog every few minutes!"

"We've got hours yet," Carly soothes her. "Just try the usual holding your breath and see if that works. If not, I'm sure someone will delight in trying to scare them out of you."

Laura actually looks around as if trying to catch someone at it, and everyone falls about laughing.

Zoe is nervous. She didn't think she would be, after all, it's everything she's ever dreamed of. And more.

I can't believe my dad will actually be walking me down the aisle. Even mum seems pleased about that, now that she's gotten over the shock of his sudden return anyway.

"Come on ladies, the Champagne has arrived along with the breakfast trolley," Carly announces. "Just help yourselves, but don't take the food near any of the dresses. PJ's and dressing-gowns only while eating!"

All but those being tended by the hair and beauty team head towards the buffet style breakfast that the wait staff is laying out.

Heated stainless steel dishes are filled with freshly cooked lean bacon rashers, another with tomatoes, and others with scrambled eggs, waffles, croissants and mushrooms. And for those who don't want a cooked breakfast there is toast and a variety of cereals.

"Good heavens," Rose exclaims when she eyes the feast, "if we eat all this we'll never fit into our clothes. Don't eat all of that," she tells Laura, "your dress will never fit!"

Poor Laura looks at her plate of bacon, tomatoes,

scrambled eggs and mushrooms with a wistful longing.

"Don't mind Rose," Carly whispers in Laura's ear, "my sister always has been a bit of a bossy boots. It won't do you any harm, you've got plenty of time till you need to put your dress on."

But the thought of her beautiful dress looking tight on her makes Laura offer the plate to the next in line.

The last thing she wants is for Connor to see her looking bloated. Laura is very much in love with Palmer's brother and best man, and wants him to be impressed when she walks towards him up the aisle behind Zoe.

"Ok, Jake you're having a little trim," his mother, Stella, tells him, taking the boy's hand and leading him over to the waiting hairdresser.

"What do you think?" Carly asks, showing Zoe her new manicure. "I've never had my nails professionally done before."

"They look lovely – though I'm not sure they'll be able to do anything with mine," she tells her mother, holding her hands behind her back as she used to when she was a little girl.

"Oh, Zoe, don't tell me you've been biting your nails again. Not right before your wedding!"

"Not to worry," the manicurist smiles reassuringly. "I can work miracles with this lot," she says, waving a hand over her table of equipment. "And we've got plenty of time to do a proper job."

"Ok, well, that's good then," Zoe sits down at the small table, "because you've really got your work cut out!"

Carly shakes her head and walks over to her niece who is holding Jake on her knee while his hair is trimmed.

"How's it going, Stella? You are looking very handsome, young man," Carly tells the boy, and receives a very pleased smile.

"They're so good, I can take them anywhere and they behave. But one foot inside their own front door and all hell breaks loose," Stella laughs.

"I suppose we can't have it all," Carly chuckles. "And they really are adorable. I imagine they can charm their way out of trouble when needs be."

Zoe is so impressed by her nails that she makes a mental note to pay the manicurist a handsome tip. *Oh lordy, now for the hairdresser and I still haven't decided if I want my hair up or down!*

Sitting down in front of the large mirror stood on a table in front of her, Zoe looks at her own reflection and winces.

Her eyes have shadows under them and her hair, although freshly washed, looks limp and lifeless.

"I don't suppose you work miracles like the manicurist, do you?" she asks hopefully. "Look, she made my bitten off stumps look long and elegant," she tells the young stylist, turning her hands this way and that to show her.

"No problemo," the girl smiles, taking a line out of the Arnold Schwarzenegger Terminator film. "These hands are magic – now what did you have in mind?"

"Hey Zoe, a lovely bouquet of flowers just arrived for you," Laura shouts over the music that Stella has put on. "Where do you want them?"

"Just put them in my room – is there a note?" she asks, smiling apologetically through the mirror up to the stylist waiting to get started on her hair.

"Yep, but it's sealed. You want me to open it?"

"No, that's ok; just leave them in my room. I'll look later," she tells her, and smiles again at the stylist.

Only an hour to go before her wedding and Zoe looks at herself in her bedroom mirror and barely recognises the young woman looking back at her.

She hasn't put her wedding gown on yet, but the hair and make-up, and even her nails, look like something out of a glossy magazine.

If you're not impressed by me now, Palmer Johnson, you never will be!

At the back of her reflection, Zoe notices the flowers that Laura must have been on about earlier.

Crossing to them, Zoe grins and feels her cheeks blush with happiness.

A bunch of at least three dozen red roses are standing on her dressing table, a note in a beautiful holder standing at their centre.

The envelope is a bit bigger than the usual note, or card that florists use. But she assumes that Palmer will have given this to them especially.

Opening the envelope, Zoe unfolds a letter and takes out what appears to be a couple of photos.

'I warned you over and over again, but you just wouldn't believe me. Now see for yourself, bitch!'

Her knees buckle beneath her and Zoe sits down hard on the bedroom floor.

"This isn't real! This can't be real! Oh God, please, please, please, don't let this be real!"

Her hands are shaking and the photos are blurring as her eyes fill with red hot tears.

One final letter and it has been sent to Zoe on her wedding day, just a short time before she is due to become Palmer Johnson's wife!

Her sobs are deep and rob her of breath, causing her to gasp for air. She can't stop staring at the photos now fallen to the floor, and the note she still holds trembling in her hand.

How? When? Who is she? Does anyone else know? Is she the mother of the baby the other letter spoke about?

No! This isn't right! Damn it, Palmer wouldn't do this to me! This is all lies!

But the photos look back at her from the floor, clear and sharp and showing Palmer kissing another woman.

And not just a peck on the cheek. It looks to be a full on embrace. And he's wearing that blue top I like. It isn't even very old. Which means these photos aren't very old either!

Oh, God!

Her head aches and her eyes hurt and her heart is breaking in her chest.

"What do I do?" she asks the empty room, glad now that she had locked the bedroom door to get a few moments of peace and quiet. "Everyone is expecting us to get married," she cries, hauling herself up from the floor and finding a box of tissues.

Blowing her nose, Zoe tries to think.

Why didn't they send these photos to me before today? If all they wanted was to split us up, why wait until the very last moment to show them to me?

Maybe that's it? Maybe this is all just a ruse to split us up?

Turning the photos in her hand, Zoe looks at the colour prints and sees a time and date stamp on the back of each.

Falling onto the bed she curls into a foetal position and rocks herself, clutching at her stomach to stifle the unbearable pain.

A knock at the door pulls Zoe out of her well of self-pity and back to the reality of the day.

"Zoe, I think we should get your dress on, darling," her mother calls through the door. "I can give you another few minutes, but we can't leave it much longer."

"Ok, mum," Zoe manages to shout, her voice strangely normal sounding to her own ears.

It's now or never! If I go through with the marriage I'm always going to wonder. But what if it isn't true?

Again, she bends to pick up the photos and this time her quieted mind accepts the images before her.

There is no doubt, the man in the photos is Palmer and he is kissing a woman that Zoe has never met. And more importantly, someone that Palmer has never told her about.

If it was innocent he would have. There would be no reason to hide it from me. If she's an old friend or colleague, he would have told me about her, but he didn't!

Looking across the room to a door leading out of the

bedroom and directly into the hotel corridor, Zoe makes up her mind.

She pulls on the skirt and top she had worn to the hotel the night before, along with tights and shoes. Then she crosses to the door where her mother and all her wedding party are waiting for her in the private lounge, and listens to the continuing chatter.

Good. They seem occupied enough not to think about me for a while. I need to see my father!

Going out into the corridor, Zoe walks along to the next room and knocks on the door.

Her father looks handsome in his new suit, but Zoe barely notices. She pushes past him and flings herself onto the settee.

Having closed the door behind her, Douglas crosses to his daughter and pulls her into his arms.

"What the hell has happened?" he demands, holding a sobbing Zoe against his chest. "Zoe please, you need to tell me what's wrong."

But she can't. Instead she holds out her hand and lets him take the letter and photos from her.

"Bloody hell!" he explodes, his eyes bulging with disbelief. "What the fuck does that boy think he's doing — and to my daughter!" he exclaims proprietorially.

"Please, I need to get away — you said you'd stand by

me. I need your help," she tells him, her eyes pleading with him not to let her down. Not now, not when she needs him so badly. "Please, dad?"

He'd dreamed of hearing his daughter one day calling him dad. But that was all it had been, just a dream. Yet here she is, asking for his help — no, she is asking for her dads help and he won't let her down. Not ever again.

"Wait here, I'll call one of the drivers to bring a car around then we'll get you away and I'll deal with the rest," he tells her, taking charge of the situation.

And, true to his word, he smuggles Zoe out of the manor house before anyone can miss her.

"Now I'll deal with Mr Palmer Johnson!" And he rubs his hands together before going down the stairs to the hall where the wedding service is waiting to begin.

EPILOGUE

The cottage that her father has bought for her is so lovely and has a panoramic view of the river.

No one has ever thought to look for her in Cornwall, and she had begged her father not to tell anyone where she is.

She writes to her mother regularly, but always sends them to her father first and he mails them on to her mother so that the post mark doesn't give her away.

It has been 3 and a half months since the wedding fiasco and Zoe is settling into village life in Looe.

With her father's help she is able to manage on a small wage working in a local florist shop, just part-time to give her some pocket money and to keep her from fretting about the past.

"How's that arrangement coming?" Tara, the shop

owner asks Zoe as she walks over to take a look at her work. "You're a natural at this, I couldn't have done a better job myself, and I've been at this for over ten years!"

Pleased and proud, Zoe smiles up at Tara, ever thankful that the older woman had taken her on to work in the shop.

Cornish people don't always take to strangers – or 'foreigners' as the local's call outsiders. But Tara had welcomed her, once she knew that she was a permanent fixture in the village and not just passing through.

At the end of the day, Zoe turns left on Fore Street and walks past the pharmacy, then holds her nose as she hurries on past the busy fish and chip shop.

Anything greasy seems to turn her stomach lately, but she's learned to work around it.

Arriving home, she lifts down a vase and arranges the flowers that Tara allowed her to take home. They would have been wasted anyway, so it was nice that someone got some pleasure out of them.

Zoe walks out into her back garden; from here she can see the River Looe, gleaming in the early April sun.

Although the sun is still shining the temperature is cold, and Zoe shivers as the wind lifts her hair.

She pulls her cardigan tighter about her, but doesn't

go back indoors. Instead she walks among the shrubs and heathers growing in her garden, looks out at the grey-blue sky that dips down into the river.

What is it about water that is so peaceful? It could be freezing out here and I'd still love it!

Her mind calms as her eyes revel in the ethereal beauty that is Cornwall.

Green and grey, blue and yellow, the grass and heathers bend to the wind's will and dance like waves upon the land.

I should be over him, I know that, but I can't help wondering what Palmer is doing right at this minute. Has he returned to the woman in the photos? Or has he moved on to someone new?

It shouldn't matter, but somehow it still does. I wish I could say I no longer love him, but that would be a lie.

Instead I'll just tell the wind I'm grieving, and know that grieving takes time to end.

This hurt will cease in time, that's the one sure fact that keeps me going each day. Pain like this can't last forever.

But she has watched her mother grieve for many years. Hurting for the husband that had abandoned her and her daughter.

Well, how the world turns. My father is back and

without his help I wouldn't be here. Yet now I'm standing in my mother's shoes.

Her hand falls to caress her belly, barely swollen yet. But deep inside a baby is growing and Zoe now faces a future as a single parent.

It's alright, baby, we'll get by. And mummy will keep you safe and warm and happy in the years to come.

But Zoe still grieves for the life she so nearly had. For the man who had almost become her husband, and who is the father of her unborn child.

She had left his ring, along with the letter on her dressing table before leaving in the car her father had organised. But for some reason, some obscure need to keep something of him with her, she had taken the photos but had buried them deep in a drawer out of sight.

One day, maybe I will tell him that we have a child. But I doubt he will be interested.

After all, he already has one doesn't he, if the letters are to be believed. And why shouldn't I believe them, the camera never lies!

*****

If you have enjoyed this book, please take the time to leave a review on the website from where you bought it. Thank you